Crazy for Cupcakes
Delilah Horton, Book 5

Bethany Lopez

Crazy for Cupcakes
Copyright 2022 Bethany Lopez
Published July 2022
ISBN - 978-1-954655-24-9

Cover Design by Allison Martin
Editing by Red Road Editing / Kristina Circelli
Ebook Formatting by Bethany Lopez

This ebook is licensed for your personal enjoyment only. This ebook may not be re-sold or given away to other people. If you would like to share this ebook with another person, please purchase an additional copy for each recipient. If you're reading this ebook and did not purchase it, or it was not purchased for your use only, then please return to your favorite book retailer and purchase your own copy. Thank you for respecting the hard work of this author. All rights reserved.

All rights reserved. No part of this book may be reproduced, scanned, or distributed in any printed or electronic form without permission. Please don't participate in or encourage piracy of copyrighted materials in violation of the author's rights. Purchase only authorized editions.

This is a work of fiction. Names, characters, places, and incidents either are the product of the author's imagination or are used fictitiously, and any resemblance to actual persons, living or dead, businesses, companies, events, or locales is entirely coincidental.

This ebook is also available in print at most online retailers.

Want to learn more about my books? Sign up for my newsletter and Join my FB Group/Street Team!
www.bethanylopeauthor.com
https://www.facebook.com/groups/1443318612574585/

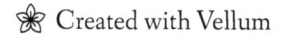

❈ Created with Vellum

For everyone who asked for more of Lila, Cade, and the whole gang. I hope you love continuing their journey with me!

Prologue

They say the first year of marriage is the *honeymoon phase*, where you tread carefully as you get to know your new roles and navigate living together as a married couple.

Lots of sex ... *check.*

Arguments over stupid shit ... *check.*

Learning how to balance work and family life ... *uh, we're still working on that one.*

And finally, dealing with an MC rivalry that has your town and its residents in the crosshairs and your new husband working overtime.

We'd returned home from our amazing European honeymoon relaxed, refreshed, and ready to kick some marital ass. I was excited to see my kids, spend time with my girls, and get back to work.

My PI agency was still relatively new and as the only show in town, we weren't hurting for clients. Luckily one of my besties, Carmen, had started working with me, which eased some of the load.

We just hadn't expected the load to get quite so heavy.

Add to that Bea, another one of our girl gang and a local cop, has a case that she's struggling to close and needs our help.

Suffice it to say life is anything but relaxing and I've been stress eating enough cupcakes to keep Amy May in business for life. If things don't slow down soon, I'm going to go crazy ... *crazy for cupcakes*!

Chapter One

"*Happy birthday to you, happy birthday, Elin and Elena, happy birthday to you.*"

"Cha cha cha," Elin said with a big smile before closing his eyes to make a wish and blowing out the candles on his cake.

I always gave the twins their own cakes with their own candles on their birthday. Sure, it meant we always had a lot of cake leftover, but I was up to the challenge.

This year, Elin had requested a cake featuring his favorite baseball team, the Chicago Cubs, while Elena had opted for a *Friends* theme. She and her best friend, Cassidy, Amy May's daughter, had recently binged the series and she was obsessed with all things Ross and Rachel.

The twins were turning twelve, so although we were having a small celebration today, on the actual date of their birth, they'd already also had their own individual birthday parties with their friends, as well as a celebration with their dad and soon-to-be stepmom, Mary.

Elin had chosen a day of paintball with his buddies, while Elena had opted for having her friends over for a sleepover. This had included movies, pizza, an at-home spa, and karaoke.

Elin's party had been much less stressful.

Luckily, Amy May had joined me for Elena's party, and we'd had our own adult sleepover, complete with margaritas and plenty of cupcakes.

"Yay!" I cried, clapping my hands together before asking, "Who wants ice cream with their cake?"

"Strawberry," Elin said.

"No thanks and just a little piece of cake," Lena replied.

"None for me," my sexy beast of a husband, Cade, said as he walked out of the room before returning seconds later with two wrapped packages.

Huh, he hadn't mentioned getting them anything. How sweet.

My heart got all squishy in that annoying *I'm in love with my new husband who's so thoughtful and hot and the perfect stepdad to my kids* kind of way.

I went into the kitchen to get Elin his strawberry, and chocolate for myself, but the sounds of the twins shouting had me running back into the dining room, ice cream scoop in hand with chocolate ice cream running down my arm.

"What happened?" I asked worriedly.

Lena held up her hand and excitedly showed me the new iPhone she was holding. I spun my head toward Elin and saw he was holding an identical phone.

"Cade ... *what the hell?*" I asked.

I knew how much those phones cost and there was no way I would have been on board with him buying them. Of course, he knew that, which was why he didn't ask.

"Swear jar," Elin said automatically.

I sighed and looked at my son.

"Aren't you getting a little old for the swear jar, honey?"

"Not as long as it's still pulling in a profit," the little wiseass replied.

It's true the swear jar had been a good source of income for the twins, especially in the last couple of years. Hell, they'd recently bought a new trampoline with their swear jar money.

"I love it so much, thank you!" Lena said as she moved to put her arms around Cade.

"You're welcome, darlin'," he replied before dropping a kiss on top of her head.

"Seriously, it's the coolest," Elin agreed, grinning up at Cade.

"I'm glad you like it, both of you."

Cade was about two-hundred-and-twenty pounds of muscle and man. Tall and gorgeous, his Hawaiian genes made for one hell of a delectable package. His hair was long and wild, unless he had it pulled back like he did right then, and his beard had been recently trimmed. With his low-slung jeans and leather vest over a white T, he looked like the motorcycle badass he was, yet the way he looked at my children... with love in his eyes and a tenderness that made my heart sing ... made him even more attractive to me.

It was hard to be mad at him when he looked like that, but I'd do my best.

"Cade, it's too much," I argued, ignoring the matching death glares that turned my way.

"Lila, *babe*, you're dripping," Cade replied, looking pointedly at where the chocolate was dripping off my elbow onto the floor.

"*Shit*," I muttered and spun to go back in the kitchen.

I heard Elin mutter, "*Swear jar*," again and rolled my eyes as I hurried to the sink.

Cade's footsteps sounded behind me seconds before his arms came around my waist.

"I wanted to get them something special for their birthday," he said softly, his lips gently brushing against the top of my ear.

"I know, Cade ... but spending over a thousand dollars on phones for twelve-year-old kids is crazy. *We* don't even have phones that expensive."

Sure, I was peeved, but that didn't stop me from leaning back against his chest and enjoying the way his heat enveloped me.

"Did you see how happy they were?" he asked, holding me tighter.

I nodded and he said, "That's all that matters. I wanted to see their faces light up ... It was a selfish gift."

I shook my head and chuckled. Sure, I knew he was playing me, but how could I argue with his logic.

Plus, we were all trying to get used to the new dynamics of our house.

"In the future, I'd appreciate it if you discussed big purchases like that with me, especially when it's for the kids. Okay?"

"I can do that," Cade said, lowering his voice so his answer was a rumble.

My body quivered in response, and I felt his lips curve up.

"I'm happy to accept any punishment you feel the need to dole out."

I dropped the ice cream scoop and turned in his arms.

"Really?"

The look in his eyes was downright smoldering as he nodded.

Pleasure zipped through me as at least a dozen possibilities ran through my brain.

"Mom, where's the ice cream?" Elin called from the other room, pulling me out of my sexual haze.

"Coming!" I yelled back, then lowered my voice and grinned up at Cade. "You'll be yelling that later."

"I look forward to it," he replied, dropping his arms and stepping back so I could turn and scoop. "And, Lila?"

I looked at him over my shoulder.

"Be creative."

And with that parting shot, he turned and went back to the kids, leaving me at the counter with my mind spinning and my pulse pounding.

Chapter Two

Now, whipped cream and cherries weren't *all that* creative, but Cade didn't seem to mind.

One of my favorite movies when I was younger had been *Varsity Blues*, and I don't know any woman who's seen it that hasn't thought about doing the old *whipped cream bikini* trick herself.

Sure, I need a little more whipped cream than the actress in the movie, and my boobs weren't quite as perky, so there was some drippage, but the look on Cade's face when I'd come walking out of the bathroom wearing nothing but cream proved it didn't matter.

"*Holy, hell, woman*, you look good enough to eat ... and that's just what I'm gonna do," he growled, prowling toward me, his hands reaching down to grasp the hem of his shirt and whip it over his head.

The good Lord and many hours of manual labor had blessed my husband with a body so delectable, no additional toppings were required.

I felt a throbbing between my legs and worried the whipped cream would melt before Cade got to it, but I should have known better. As soon as he reached me, Cade knelt down, spread my legs apart so that I had to lean back against the wall and brace myself, and moved in for his dessert.

"*Oh my God*," I moaned, my head falling back a little too hard, but I didn't mind the sudden jolt. The pain kind of added to the experience.

Cade licked me clean, then began to work me over in earnest, his fingers squeezing my ass and tilting my hips slightly upward as he pressed me closer. A little cream dripped off my breasts and onto his hair, but before I could mention it, he began flicking his tongue rapidly and I lost the ability to form words.

I squeaked and reached down to hold on his shoulders as my hips rocked against his mouth.

"That's it, baby," he murmured against me.

I felt the rumble of his words and the heat of his breath against me.

He nuzzled my clit briefly with his nose as two fingers slid inside me and began thrusting in and out. I let out a little cry as the tension began to build and was gifted with his tongue once more.

It wasn't long before I was crying out in earnest as the orgasm slammed through me and his fervor turned to lazy licks.

"Mm, looks like I missed a spot," Cade said, and although I didn't have the strength to open my eyes, I felt his mouth begin to kiss a trail over my stomach toward my breasts.

He licked and sucked until not only was I completely naked in front of him, but my libido started picking back up, as if my world hadn't been rocked moments before.

"I didn't realize you liked sweets so much," I said with a chuckle as he gathered me into his arms.

"Only when you're at the center," he said with a grin, dropping his head to crush his lips against mine.

He ravaged my mouth as he lifted me easily and walked us toward the bed.

"Want me to get the bottle to spray some on you?" I asked as I bounced on the mattress.

Cade braced himself over me and said, "The only thing I want coating my cock is your pussy ... or your mouth."

Yup, that did it, I am officially ready for round two.

"I think that can be arranged," I said with a smile as I reached between us to undo his jeans.

He quickly shucked them off, leaving no barrier between his long, hard cock and my eager hands. I grasped his length with both, curling them around him in fists and tugging as I moved up to bite his shoulder.

"Harder, babe."

I wasn't sure which he meant, so I did both ... I bit down hard and jacked his dick in a way I'd worry was too much, if his response wasn't a low, gorgeous groan.

I pushed him then, not hard enough to do much of anything, since he outweighed me by like a hundred pounds, but enough to get him to do what I wanted, which was lay back and let me have my way with him.

As soon as he was prone, I positioned myself between his legs and bent over to slide my mouth over his cock, sucking my cheeks in as I pumped the base in tandem.

His hand moved over my hair gently, before moving down to cup my breast and fondle the nipple. *Thank God for those long-ass arms*, I thought as I tried to focus on what I was doing and not the wonderful *zing* that ran down me when he pinched and twisted.

"Enough," Cade said gruffly, which I knew meant he was close to coming and he didn't want to come in my mouth. So, I gave him one last lick and sat back on my knees, my gaze rapt on his handsome face. "Turn around and get on your knees."

"*Yes, sir,*" I said jauntily, practically falling off the bed in my effort to get quickly in position.

My sex life with my ex-husband had been predictable and often boring, but since I'd met Cade, I'd been anything but bored. I didn't know if it was our chemistry, our love, or both, but never in my life had I experienced anything like I did with him.

He gave my hip a loving caress as I dropped my face to the bed and turned to rest on my cheek.

My body surged forward as he entered me quickly, a gasp escaping my lips as I widened my legs even farther to accommodate him. His thrusts were fast and deep, and I knew it wouldn't last too long after the teasing he'd endured. I reached between my legs to find my clit, but Cade beat me to it.

Happy to just enjoy the ride, I dropped my hand and grasped the comforter tightly as Cade drove us both into a frenzy and then over the edge.

Chapter Three

"*Hello, hello.*"

"Back here!" I shouted back in response.

I'd known Carmen was coming by this morning, so I'd left the front door unlocked after the kids went to school and Cade left for work. Cade hated it when I did that, but I knew I'd be busy in the makeshift office on our screened-in porch, so I did it anyway.

"I'm thinking it's time for a move," I called out to Carmen just as she walked into the room. "Oh, sorry for yelling. I didn't realize you were so close."

"It's all good, how are you?" she asked sunnily as she practically bounced from the door to my desk. "And what do you mean, move? Are you guys looking for a new place? I thought you loved it here … What about Cade's cabin?"

She was a little like Tigger, always excited and bouncy. And she often spoke at a rapid-fire pace.

I grinned at her and took a sip from my coffee mug before replying.

"We *are* happy here, and with Cade's cabin. We may move eventually … But I was talking about moving to a real office space. Now that there are two of us full time, I think we could use the extra room."

"Oh, that would be cool. Do you have a location in mind?" Carmen asked as she settled into the seat across from me.

"Probably downtown Greenswood, or as close to downtown as we could get. A small commercial space should do the trick. Something with enough room for us to work and have clients come in if needed. I'd feel better about having them meet us in a dedicated office space, rather than here or the library."

"Do you want me to start looking? You know how much I love research."

I did know that. In fact, I'd been banking on it.

"That would be great," I replied happily. "If you take care of that, I'll get started on this case that came in last night. It's your standard cheating case, so I should be able to close it out in no time."

I looked up to see Carmen's lower lip sticking out prettily.

"Why are you pouting? I thought you'd be excited about looking for real estate."

"I am, it's just ... I love a good cheating case," she said, her voice just a smidge away from a whine. "And Bran has been making me work out every morning, so I wanted to put my newfound stamina to use."

Branson Braswell was a good friend and Carmen's new steady squeeze.

"Better you than me," I muttered. I used to spend my mornings working out with Bran and to say he was dedicated in the gym would be an understatement. Just thinking about it made my legs sore. "And don't worry, there will be plenty more cheating cases. The world is full of cheating bastards, of every gender."

"I know," Carmen replied, still sounding dejected.

"Everything good with you and Bran?" I asked.

They'd only been back from their trip to Hawaii for a few weeks and things between them seemed to be heating up, but I know when things started Carmen had been pretty nervous about their compatibility, so it didn't hurt to ask.

Carmen's face lit up, which gave me my answer.

"Yeah, things are great. So great, in fact, it's kind of scary. I never knew guys like him existed, ya know? He's so sweet and attentive ... and sexy. I mean, sometimes I catch myself just looking at him and thinking ... *damn*! I just worry it's too good to be true."

I got up and rounded my desk to lean against it. I crossed my arms over my chest to stop myself from shaking her.

"Carmen, we've been over this. You and Bran have been over this. When are you going to realize your worth and stop torturing yourself?"

She bit her lip and said, "I know, I know ... I just can't seem to stop the doubts from creeping in."

"Bran loves you."

Carmen nodded. "I know he does."

"So, trust him."

"I do."

"And, hey, we all have those feelings. There are so many times I look at Cade and wonder what the hell he's doing with me. I mean, he's seriously hot and a total badass. He could get any woman he wants. Then I realize ... he wants me, so I must be pretty special too. At least to him."

"You are. He totally loves you."

"And Bran totally loves *you*."

Carmen stood up and threw her arms around my waist, pulling me in for a tight squeeze.

"Thanks, Lila."

"Anytime, babe," I replied. "Now, I'm gonna head out. You gonna be cool here on your own?"

"Yuppers."

I picked up the file on my newest client and walked through the house.

Carmen had been working on getting our files to be completely digital, but I was having a hard time with the transition. Sure, it was quicker, more efficient, and saved trees, but there was something comforting to me about being able to open a folder and look through my notes.

I guess you could say I had a hard time with change.

Once I was in my Caravan, I started it up and pointed it toward downtown. The clock on my dash said I had just enough time for a pit stop at Amy May's Bakery for some cupcakes before I got down to business and caught myself some cheaters.

Perfect.

Chapter Four

"Hello, beautiful. Wow, aren't you gorgeous," I cooed to the banana nut cupcake with whipped cream cheese frosting in my hand.

"You have issues," Amy May said as she lowered herself into the booth across from me.

She was due to pop in two weeks, so it took a bit of effort.

"And you love me for it," I quipped, then took the first delectable bite.

"*Mmmmm God,*" I moaned as the flavors exploded on my tongue. "I've said it before, and I'll say it again ... You're a goddess."

"A goddess who can't shave her legs or tie her own

shoes," she replied with a sigh. "I'm so ready to get this baby out of me. He's sucking the life right out of me."

Her hair was coming loose, so Amy May pulled out the rubber band and worked on putting it back up in a ponytail as I scarfed down the rest of her creation.

She did look tired. Even though it had been a while since I'd had the twins, I still remembered how tough the last few weeks of pregnancy were, and if I was honest, I was glad it was Amy May dealing with it and not me.

I didn't think I'd ever want to go through the whole deal again ... pregnancy, infants, toddlers. I mean, sure, I may not have twins again, but I didn't think I was in a place in my life where I wanted to start over, even with only one kid.

Luckily, Cade wasn't jonesing for a baby. On the flip side, his mother *had* been hinting at more grandchildren even before we'd gotten engaged and made sure to work kids into the conversation every time we talked.

Thankfully, Cade's parents lived in Hawaii, so the pressure wasn't too heavy.

"Just a few more weeks," I assured her.

"Easy for you to say," she said with a grimace. "You're not the one with hemorrhoids who pees a little every time she laughs or coughs."

"Hey, I had twins," I argued. "I pee my pants all the time."

Amy May chuckled and shook her head.

"The stuff women have to deal with, am I right?"

"That you are, sister," I agreed, putting my hands on the table and pushing myself up to stand. "I hate to run out on you, but I've got a case. You gonna be all right?"

Her lips turned up briefly.

"Yeah, I'm down to half days now. I've beefed up my staff and they've really been coming through for me. Jason wants me to stop working altogether, but I think I've got at least another week of half days, then maybe I'll take a short break before the baby comes."

"Let me know if you need anything," I said, bending to drop a kiss on her head before turning for the door. "I'm just a phone call away."

"I know, thanks. And be careful out there."

"Always," I shot back and headed out.

Chapter Five

Cheaters had been my bread and butter for the last few years. It all started when I'd caught my then-husband cheating in the Applebee's parking lot, took a picture, and posted it all over town. This had made Moose, the only PI in town, contact me about taking pictures for him.

I'd happily taken the job and found it to be something I enjoyed. Sure, I'd gotten myself into some pickles, some quite dangerous ... one of which that had cost Moose his life.

He'd left me his business in the will, and I'd taken over the PI duties. Now, although I had Carmen to help me out, I found myself wondering how he'd done it all by himself before I'd come along.

Now I was the only PI in our tri-city area and

although our population wasn't that high, you'd be surprised at how many cases came across my desk each day. Not all cheaters ... I'd covered theft, missing persons, and heck, even murder ... but, sad to say, it was mostly cheaters.

Why people couldn't simply be honest and leave a relationship they were unhappy in rather than hurting each other and ultimately ruining families, I'd never understand.

This latest piece of work was a teacher at the local high school, and her husband was worried she was having an affair with another teacher who she hung out with all the time. He'd contacted me via the new website I was rockin', thanks to Carmen, and had even Cash App'd the money over right away before the job was even done.

I appreciated the gesture, and although I hoped he was wrong about his wife, I'd have an answer for him by the end of the day.

I pulled into the parking lot of the Greenswood Motel and drove around the back, where I saw the car my client had described as his wife's.

I parked a few spaces away and waited.

After a few moments of diligently watching the windows and doors of the motel for any sign of movement, my phone rang. I saw Bea's name flash on the screen and answered it, never taking my eyes off the building.

"Hey, babe, what's up?" I asked before she could speak.

"Hey, Lila," she replied, her tone harried. "Do you think we could meet up later, maybe on my lunch break? I have this case that's driving me nuts and I'd like to get your take on it. Maybe talking it out with you will help..."

I pulled the phone back to look at the screen once more, needing to assure myself it was actually *Bea* who'd called me. It wasn't that she didn't think I could do my job, but as local law enforcement, she usually preferred I let her, and her people, handle the crime in Greenswood. Especially if they were dangerous, which, I must admit, were usually the kind I ended up getting tangled in.

"Really?" I asked, once I double checked the name and number. "You *want* my help?"

"Yeah, this one's got us chasing our tails and I really need to find out what's happening."

Intrigued, and flattered that she'd asked, I said, "Of course. Just let me know when and where and I'll be there. You want me to pull Carmen in too?"

"Sure, that would be great. The more minds the better."

"Okay, we'll be there."

"Thanks, Lila."

"Anytime."

I disconnected just as a young guy got out of the backseat of an old Chevy, leaned back in to say something to the dude who was driving, and then pulled back with a laugh and smacked the hood of the car.

The car drove off, leaving the boy, who I was guessing was seventeen, tops. He sauntered toward the door with the number twelve on it and raised his hand to knock.

I grabbed my long lens camera as the door opened and a pretty brunette with a saucy bob and red lipstick reached out to grab the boy by his shirt and pull him quickly inside before shutting the door behind him. But not before I snapped at least a dozen shots.

I looked down at the picture of my client's wife and sighed.

She wasn't having an affair with another teacher; she was sleeping with a student.

I stayed for an hour and got some pictures of them leaving the room, the woman's lipstick no longer intact and the boy looking disheveled and utterly pleased with himself.

The woman left first, and I got a shot of her license plate, then waited for the boy to be picked back up by his buddy, who gave him a high five before peeling out of the parking lot.

As a woman, I was a little impressed someone my age could find time to balance work, a family, and an affair with someone with the stamina of a horny rabbit. As a mother, I was disgusted, horrified, and determined to take the bitch down.

I called Carmen as I drove away from the motel.

"Hey, Car, it's me. Just wanted to let you know that Bea wants to meet up with us over lunch to get our take on one of her cases. I'm finished with the cheater … just got to write up my notes and send them off to my client along with the photos. How're you doin'?"

"Great," she replied cheerfully. "I'm downtown on Main Street now, about to meet up with a realtor. Just text me where you want me to meet you guys and I'll be there."

"Wow, you're with a realtor already?"

"Yuppers. I let her know we're serious buyers and need a place asap, so she jumped to help us."

"Great. I knew I could count on you," I said, and I had. If I'd left it for myself to handle, it would have taken me at least a week to even look up a realtor's phone number.

"Aww, thanks, Lila."

My phone dinged and I said, "Just a sec ... Okay, Bea wants to meet us at Jake's in thirty. Does that work?"

"I'll make it work," she promised, and I grinned.

"If anyone can, it's you. See you there."

"See ya!"

Chapter Six

Bea was already seated in a booth when I got there, so I leaned down to give her a kiss on the top of her head before sliding in across from her.

"Hey, lady," I said easily, frowning when I noticed how pale she looked, and the dark circles under her eyes. "You good?"

Bea took a sip of her coffee then set down the cup before letting out a soft sigh.

"Yeah ... you know ... work and stuff."

I frowned, not sure if she was telling me everything but not wanting to press when she was in uniform, and we were here to consult on a case.

"Okay ... you know you can call me anytime, come over anytime."

She gave me a small smile and nodded. "I do know that. Thanks."

"Chocolate cake and fries, Lila?" the server asked as she approached.

I should probably be embarrassed that my standing order sounded more like a child's than a woman in her thirties, but what can I say ... *the stomach wants what the stomach wants.*

"And a Coke, please."

Bea grimaced. "How can you put all that in your body?"

I nodded at her mug and said, "We can't all live on coffee alone."

"Hey, guys," Carmen said as she bounded up to our table and told me to "Scooch." "Sorry I took so long, but I really think I've found the perfect place. Lila, you have to go and see it. The realtor said she'd be available later this evening if you wanted to stop by. Her name's Staci, *with an I.*"

"Realtor?" Bea asked.

"For an office," I told her as Carmen picked up a menu.

"Man, I really want the nachos, but I feel guilty eating that after working out. I should probably get a salad," Carmen said, sounding glum.

"What's the point of working out if not so you can

eat what you want?" I asked.

"Health. Fitness. A longer life," Bea supplied.

I stuck my tongue out at her and the knot in my stomach eased a bit when she grinned in response.

"The heck with it, I'm getting the nachos," Carmen said with a decisive nod and told our server when she came back with my fries.

"Atta girl," I replied, dipping a fry generously in ketchup as I looked to Bea and asked, "So, what's the case?"

"It's these car jackings," she began, frustration written all over her face. "We've had three so far. Out-of-towners driving really nice cars – a BMW, a Tesla, and a Porsche. They all said they got lost, even though they were using GPS, then got a flat tire, and when they get out to check the tire, they're knocked out. When they come to, they're in an alley a couple blocks from the Greenswood Hospital and have no idea how they got there."

"All three exactly the same?" I asked, furrowing my brow as I tried to piece together what she was saying.

"Exactly," Bea replied.

"So, they were using GPS and still ended up in the wrong place, or exactly the right place for whoever's jacking the cars."

Bea nodded and Carmen muttered, "That's

bonkers."

"We tried going to all three victims' intended locations, hoping there'd be some sort of tie-in or similarity, or maybe we'd be able to retrace their steps, but there's no correlation at all. And when we plugged the addresses into our GPS, it led us right to their destination. No issues."

"That's really strange."

"I know," Bea said, with a tired sigh. "It's got us scratching our heads ... and you know how much I hate that."

"You sure I can't get you anything else?" our server asked Bea as she dropped off Carmen's nachos and my cake.

"No, I'm good. Thanks."

"You should probably eat," I told her. I didn't like the vibe she was giving off. Bea was always strong, take-charge, and optimistic. Especially when it came to the job.

She shook her head and said, "Nah. My stomach's too upset right now."

"So, what do you need from us?" I asked, biting back a moan at the first taste of chocolaty deliciousness.

Yes, I'd already had a cupcake today, but really that was nobody's business but my own.

"Honestly," Bea began, throwing her hands up. "I'm

not a hundred percent sure. Maybe getting another couple sets of eyes on the case will help? Maybe you'll think of something we haven't ... I don't know. All I know is that so far, they aren't targeting locals, so maybe they're local. There's been no chatter about anyone selling off the parts, but you may have better luck finding that out than me, since most people selling hot parts stay off police radar whenever possible."

"Okay, we'll keep an ear out and see if there's anything. Can we look at the files?"

Bea gave a half shrug and said, "There's not much to them, but yeah. Anything that'll help. They've all happened within the last week, so I'm guessing the car jackers will be pretty confident since they haven't gotten caught. I'm afraid they're going to keep going as long as they're making a profit and getting away with it."

"We'll help in any way we can," I said, reaching across the table to take her hand.

"Thanks, Lila," she replied.

"I think I've got something that may cheer you up."

"What's that?"

"How about someone you can arrest on statutory rape charges?" I offered, then told her about the case and showed her the pictures.

"Don't worry. I'll take care of it," she said, and I was happy to see her looking a bit more like herself.

Chapter Seven

"Carmen said this place is perfect, so I asked the realtor to meet us here really quick before dinner. If it's what I want, I'd like to move forward with it as soon as possible."

"Whatever you need, babe," Cade said as we walked down Main Street and turned the corner to where the office Carmen had recommended was located.

It was just halfway down a side street, which was fine. The best part was that it was only a short walk to Amy May's Bakery, which meant not only could I pop in on my friend, but ... unlimited access to cupcakes!

There was an attractive brunette standing in front of the building in a pretty pink skirt and jacket, her head down as she looked at her phone.

At the sound of our approach her head flew up, she

dropped her phone in her large purse, and was quick to give us a smile. It was big, almost too toothy, and if I'm honest, a bit predatory. Especially when she noticed the big hunk of man walking next to me.

I narrowed my eyes, and she must have noticed, because she softened the smile and held out her hand to me.

"You must be Delilah."

"And you must be Staci ... *with an I*."

Okay, I can admit that came out a bit snarky, but she did start it by ogling my man. My husband. I was still getting used to saying that.

Cade gave my hand a gentle squeeze, probably to tell me to tone down the bitchy. So, I placed my hand in hers and gave it a quick shake.

"Carmen said we needed to see the space, so here we are."

Staci blinked but didn't miss a beat as she moved to open the door then gestured for us to walk inside.

"Yes, Carmen, who's a delight, told me what you're looking for and as soon as she did, I thought of this building. The location is great and there's plenty of room with two separate offices, admin out front, a private bathroom, and a space that could be a perfect breakroom."

I glanced around front as she gave her spiel, while Cade walked off to look at the rest of the office.

It would need fresh paint, but other than that it looked well kept.

I could envision a couple comfy chairs with a coffee table that would serve as the waiting area, with a counter for check-in. I'm sure Carmen would have ideas of décor and ways to pretty it up.

"Why don't you have a look around and let me know what you think," Staci suggested.

I nodded to her and walked down the hall to the check out the rest of the rooms.

I found Cade in what would be the break room. When I entered, he glanced over and pointed to the wall.

"We could put a fridge there, then install a countertop next to it and a sink just there, where those pipes are. There'd be enough room for a four-top dining table..."

"It's a good size and I can see how it would work perfectly," I admitted. "I think all it needs is paint and furniture and it could be a real space."

I crossed to him and placed my arms around his waist as I looked up into his face, which still never ceased to turn me on.

"I could make you a sign for out front. *Horton Private Investigations*," he said softly.

"I was thinking it could be *Wilkes Private Investigations*."

"Yeah?" he asked with a grin.

"I'm your old lady, aren't I?" I asked, batting my eyelashes up at him.

"Careful," he growled. "Or we'll end up shocking Staci with an I out of her pantyhose."

"Don't threaten me with a good time," I replied saucily.

Cade growled again then lowered his head and kissed me breathless.

"You knew I was taking your name," I whispered when I could talk again.

"I didn't know you were changing the name of your business too. But thank you. I like you being proud of it … of me."

"Always," I assured him.

"Oh, sorry," Staci said from the doorway.

Still in Cade's arms, I turned to look at her and said, "I'll take it."

Staci's smile was genuine this time when she said, "Perfect, I'll put the offer together and we'll get it to the owner."

I looked back at Cade and asked, "Ready to eat?"

His grin was wolfish when he said, "*Always*," which made heat flood *all* of my womanly parts.

"I meant dinner with Bran and Carmen," I said, my voice husky.

He simply winked as I let him go and brought my hand up to his lips.

"Let's go, darlin'."

I left Staci with the promise that I would look over and digitally sign everything she sent that evening so we could get the offer in ASAP. She said such a prime location was sure to go quickly.

I'd need to get either Carmen or one of my kids to help me figure out the digital signing thing, but Staci didn't need to know that.

We walked back to Cade's bike, and he handed me my helmet.

"Happy?" he asked.

"Honestly, Cade, I never realized it was possible to be this happy," I admitted. Between finding and marrying him, the twins being mostly great kids, the best friends a girl could have, and a job I enjoyed and was able to make a living at, I felt well and truly blessed.

Which is why I should have been worried. Nobody's life could be so perfect, could it?

Chapter Eight

"Elin! Don't forget to take the trash out before you go get on your game," I called out as I loaded up the dishwasher.

I heard his grumbled response but couldn't make out the words. *Honestly, it's probably better that way.*

Elin shuffled behind me in silence and pulled the bag out of the can.

I heard the front door open and close, and looked back at him in confusion.

"Did Lena or Cade leave?" I asked him, but he simply shrugged and continued tying off the bag.

Before I could call out to see who was there, Alani, Cade's sister, came rushing in.

"Alani? I didn't know you were coming over," I said with a smile. She'd moved here to go to school and was staying out at Cade's cabin. We'd told her she was welcome here, but she'd been excited at the idea of being on her own.

Still, Cade had bought her a used car to use for school and she often came over when she got bored or wanted food.

"I'm sorry, they wanted it to be a surprise," she managed, her breath coming out in pants.

"Who?"

No sooner had the words left my mouth than the front door banged open, and I heard a very familiar voice yell, "Aloha, 'Ohana, come give Tūtū a hug!"

I gasped, my eyes flying to Alani. "Your parents are here?"

She nodded swiftly, causing her long black hair to fall in her face.

"Yay!" Elin cried, dropping the garbage on the kitchen floor before running into the living room to see Cade's parents.

"When?" I managed, my mind reeling.

It really seemed like they'd just left. They'd come in for the wedding and stayed with the kids while Cade and I were on our honeymoon, and only could have been back home in Hawaii for two months. Three tops.

"They just showed up at the cabin an hour ago,"

Alani replied. "I nearly had a heart attack when they walked in."

"Ma?" I heard Cade call out seconds before his footsteps rained down the stairs.

"Yes, Hiapo."

I wonder how long I can hide in the kitchen.

It wasn't that I didn't love Cade's parents. I really did. And their inclusiveness of Elin and Lena, *and me*, was amazing. But sometimes his mom didn't have a filter, and she let me know as often as possible how badly she'd like to hold a grandbaby in her arms.

"Why didn't you say you were coming?" Cade asked. "I would have picked you up from the airport."

"Your mother insisted it be a surprise," I heard his dad reply.

"You don't need to fuss over us. We'll stay with Alani at the cabin," his mom added.

Alani's eyebrows shot up at this information.

I bit back a chuckle but couldn't stop the grin from spreading across my face.

"Where's that beautiful wife of yours?" she asked. "You put a baby in her yet?"

My mouth dropped open at that and this time it was Alani who grinned.

I could hear Cade's chuckle and immediately wanted to do him bodily harm.

"Darlin'?" he called out, and Elin replied, "She's in the kitchen."

The little shit.

"You're coming with me," I said, grabbing Alani's arm and pulling her along with me.

"Hey," I called cheerfully as we entered the living room. "What a surprise!" And I was immediately engulfed in a warm hug that smelled of perfume and something that reminded me of salami.

"There she is. Lila, you look as lovely as ever," Cade's mom said as she released me from the hug but kept her hands on my biceps.

Alani struggled to get out of my grip, but I held on tight.

"Thank you, so do you. Did you have a nice flight?"

"They never give you enough food anymore. Just some silly pretzels and wafers. Who can survive on that? This time I packed some sandwiches."

That explains the salami.

"Let go and let me get in there," Cade's dad told his wife, who reluctantly released me so I could be pulled into a bear hug.

"It's nice to see you again, Pops," I said, letting myself lean into the hug a bit.

There was something about Cade's dad that made my heart go squishy.

"You too, Kuʻuipo."

"You guys hungry?" Cade asked his parents.

"I wouldn't say no to a nice meal," his mom replied.

"I could eat," his dad agreed.

"Elin, go grab Lena," I said. "She must have her ear buds in or something."

"I'll get her," Alani said, slipping out of my grasp and bolting for the stairs.

I crossed to Cade and put my arm around his waist. "Where do you want to go eat?"

He looked to his dad and asked, "What do you think, Pops, steak?"

His dad nodded in agreement and Cade glanced down at me. "Does that work?"

"Sounds good to me."

"You said you wanted to talk to me about a new case?"

"It can wait. Let's spend time with your folks, I'm sure they won't be here long..."

"Actually," his mom began. "We're gonna buy a house here in town."

I blinked up at Cade, sure I was hearing things, but when he grinned broadly, I knew I'd heard right.

"What?" I asked, my head swiveling toward her. "What about Hawaii?"

She waved her hand and said, "We'll keep the house

there, too, but with you all living here and now Alani, too, we want to be close. We figure we'll split our time between the two. That way we get time with our grandkids."

"What?" Lena asked excitedly from the top of the stairs. "You're moving here?"

She squealed and ran down the stairs and straight into Pops' arms. Elin followed and hugged Cade's mom.

Alani stood a couple steps up looking horrified. But seeing how happy my kids were, I knew having them close by would be great for the twins.

I looked back up at Cade and said, "We need to stop and get some cupcakes, and the ingredients for Loco Moco!"

Chapter Nine

"Amy May, don't you dare even *think* about lifting anything," I warned my best friend, who was so pregnant I didn't even know why she bothered getting out of bed. I would totally be laid up having my husband and kids waiting on me and keeping me as comfortable as possible.

Amy May, however, was still sneaking into the bakery to check on things, and when she saw us moving into my new office space, she'd stopped in to help out.

"I can still do stuff," she replied with a pout.

"Not on my watch, sister," I retorted. "You just sit on the comfy chair and put your feet up on the coffee table. I'm gonna call Jason and tell him to come get you."

"Traitor," she muttered, but I ignored her ire and poured her a cup of water from my new dispenser.

"Here," I said as I handed her the disposable cup, my tone gentling. "You can dictate from right there. Tell the guys where to put stuff and make sure the pictures they hang are straight."

Amy May nodded, appeased over getting a task.

I got it. I remembered the misery of those last few weeks of pregnancy, and knew she just wanted to feel normal again.

"Oh my gosh, I love my new office furniture so much," Carmen said as she bounced out of the room that would be her office. "It's so pretty and clean. I can't wait to organize it."

"You can organize mine too, if you want."

"Yay!" she said, clapping her hands together before turning and bouncing back into her space. I couldn't help but smile at her exuberance.

Thank God she was such a type A, OCD personality, because I absolutely *was not*.

"Babe, the sign's here, you want them to hang it out front?" Cade asked from the entrance.

"Yes, please," I replied, then followed him outside so I could see it.

One of the guys in Cade's MC worked with metal and offered to make me a custom sign for the office.

"Oh, that's beautiful, Pretty Boy, thanks so much," I cooed as I saw the 3D sign he'd made.

Pretty Boy, who got the nickname due to his almost ethereal good looks, blushed slightly at my praise.

I left them, knowing they'd have it handled, and went back inside to make sure the furniture movers were putting things where I wanted them.

I was moving down the hall when I heard a voice call, "Lila, where are you, Ku'uipo?" and turned on my heel to go back out into the front to greet Cade's mom.

"How are you feeling, Amy May?" she was asking as I approached.

"Ready for this baby to make its appearance," Amy May said tiredly.

"Well, anytime you need a babysitter, you let me know."

Amy May gave her a grateful smile. "That's right, Lila said you guys were getting a place here."

"Yes, and here's the business card for Staci, the realtor that found us this place," I told Ma, handing her the card. "I'm sure she'll be able to help you."

"Thank you," she said, dropping it into her massive purse. "Now, don't let me bother you, I'm just going to show myself around."

I moved through the space, popping my head in each area to see how everything looked. My adrenaline was pumping, and I felt excitement charging through me a little more in each room.

It was all coming together even better than I'd expected, and I couldn't wait to come in the next day to start my first day in my new business space. It made me feel like more of a professional, rather than someone who was still figuring things out. Even though I was. Each day brought something new, and I couldn't help but wonder what Moose was thinking when he left me his PI business.

The thought of Moose made me stop and smile, as I imagined the look on his face if he saw this place. He probably would have told me to save my money and keep it in the back of the house, just like he had, but I still think he'd be impressed.

I walked back into the break room, running my hand over the custom counter Cade had built and pausing to sit at the high-top table we'd bought. My stomach grumbled and, figuring I wasn't the only one who was hungry, pulled out my phone to order a bunch of pizzas for everyone.

"Mrs. Wilkes?"

It took a moment for it to register that the man was talking to me. I was still getting used to my married name, and with Cade's mom around, I always assumed people were addressing her.

"Yes," I replied, coming out of the chair.

"We've unloaded everything except the counter and wanted to check with you on the placement of it."

"Sure, follow me," I said, leading him back out into the front and pointing to the large space by the left wall. "Right over there."

He nodded and turned to go back out to the truck.

"I figured that was where you'd want it, but wanted to be sure," Amy May called.

"Are you hungry?" I asked as I crossed to her.

"Always," she replied with a chuckle, her hand moving to caress her stomach.

"I ordered pizza. They should be here soon."

"Perfect," she said, lifting her hand in my direction. "Help me up?"

"Of course."

Amy May got to her feet with a groan and took a couple steps.

"I was getting stiff," she said, and then looked down in shock. "Oh no ... my water just broke all over your new carpet."

"What?" I cried, then called out, "Everyone, come quickly, Amy May is in labor!"

Carmen and Cade's mom came rushing out of Carmen's office and Cade stepped inside.

"Cade, call Jason and let him know to call the doctor and meet us at the hospital," I ordered, going into *mom mode.* "Carmen, pull the van around. Ma, call Bea and Shannon, and Cynthia, and let them know." *Ma had their numbers from when they helped out with my wedding.* "Amy May, breathe…"

Everyone sprang into action as I took Amy May by the arm and led her outside.

"We're going to have to go, but I'll come back and lock up later," I told the moving guys as we shuffled out of their way.

Just then the pizza delivery guy pulled up next to the curb.

"Shoot, stay right here," I said, leaving Amy May to meet the guy as he pulled out the pizzas. "Here," I said, shoving some money at him and taking the pizzas.

As I passed Amy May, I said, "I'm just gonna leave these inside for the movers. Be right back."

"Wait," she replied. "Bring one back so we can eat it on the way. You know once I get to the hospital, they won't let me eat or drink anything."

"You got it," I said, then, knowing we'd have a full van, I grabbed two and hurried back outside so we could get loaded up and go to the hospital.

Chapter Ten

We'd basically taken over the waiting room. So much so that I felt bad for the other people who were there waiting on their own tiny miracles.

Jason was back in the delivery room with Amy May, while their daughter Cassidy was in the corner with Lena and Alani. Alani was keeping her distracted and they were all huddled over her phone watching something that had them all laughing.

Elin was sitting between Cade's parents, who I insisted didn't have to wait, but Cade's mom said she didn't want to miss out on the excitement, so there they were.

Cade and Bran were sitting next to each other, and I think they'd actually even spoken to each other a few times, which was a big deal. There was a lot of history between the two of them, but at my wedding reception Bran had gone up to Cade and buried the hatchet, and although I wouldn't call them *friends*, they were at least *friendly* now.

Bea, Shannon, and Carmen were all together, with Carmen leading the conversation, and I noticed that Bea still looked really stressed and tired, which worried me. And I promised myself I'd touch base with her again later once I was done pacing the tri-colored carpet of the waiting room.

"*Uh, this is taking too long,*" I muttered, too quiet for anyone to hear me, but needing to say the words out loud.

"Hey, hey!" I looked toward the entrance to see Cynthia standing there holding a big bakery box. "I stopped by Amy May's Bakery for provisions."

Cynthia's eyes widened when I pounced, but rather than bolt, she opened the box so I could see inside.

Cynthia was the newest member of our friend group. She was the owner of Cynthia's Coffee and Books and ordered pastries for her shop from Amy May. But we'd all met when I'd taken a case to find out who was stealing from her store.

With her wild, curly hair, long flowing skirts, and

massive amounts of eclectic jewelry, she had the look of a hippie with the heart of an angel.

"Thank you," I said, my mouth full of pineapple upside down cupcake.

"Don't talk with your mouth full," Cade's mom admonished as she joined us.

"Sorry," I managed, covering my mouth.

"What a lovely idea, Cynthia, thank you," she told Cynthia, who beamed in response.

"Anything for you, Mama Wilkes."

Before I could snag another pastry, Jason came rushing in, a huge smile on his face.

"You aren't going to believe this ... It's a girl!" he cried.

"What?" was the question that rang around the room.

We'd had Amy May's baby shower a month ago, and since she'd been told during the ultrasound it was a boy, everything we'd gotten her had been with that in mind.

"I know," Jason said with a chuckle. "Believe me, we were surprised too. You can see the baby in the nursery window, and, Lila, Amy May wants to see you. Cassidy, I'll take you back with me. Do you want to see your sister or mom first?"

"Mom," she said as she got to her feet.

"You got it," he said, holding out her arms, which she

ran into. After her gave her a big hug and kissed the top of her head, he met my eyes and asked, "Ready?"

I shoved the remainder of the cupcake in my mouth and nodded.

I followed him through the double doors and down the hallway until we got to the room with their name on the door.

Jason opened it and called, "We're back," and we walked in past a bathroom and around a closed curtain. He pushed the curtain all the way back so the room opened up, and there was Amy May on the bed.

I let out a deep breath and felt my nerves balance out. Sure, I'd figured she'd be okay, since there'd been nothing wrong with her first pregnancy, but the truth was, we weren't getting any younger, and I'd been worried anyway.

"You look beautiful," I told her as Cassidy rushed over and carefully went in for a hug.

"I feel like I just gave birth to a watermelon," she said with a tired smile. "The head on this kid…"

"Quite a surprise, huh?" I said with a chuckle as I moved to her other side and took her hand in mine.

"A good one, though."

"You want me to arrange for things to be returned?" I offered.

Amy May shook her head and said, "Nah, it doesn't

really matter the first few months anyway. We'll put a bow on her head."

"What are you going to name her?"

They'd decided on Charlie, after Amy May's dad, for the boy's name.

She shared a loving look with Jason and said, "We're keeping Charlie."

I squeezed her hand and said, "I love it."

The door opened and a nurse came in pushing a mobile bassinet into the room.

"Here we are, Mom, all cleaned up," she said as she left it next to the bed.

"Aww," Cassidy cooed, looking down into the bassinet and caressing her sister's cheek softly. "Hi, Charlie. I'm your big sis."

"You wanna hold her?" Jason asked, and Cassidy nodded eagerly.

"Go have a seat in the chair and put your arms like this," he said, as he demonstrated how he wanted her to hold them.

She did as instructed, and he picked up Charlie and placed her in Cassidy's arms.

"How are you feeling? Hungry? Do you need anything?" I asked my best friend.

Amy May laid her head back on the pillow and looked up at me.

"Just tired," she said happily.

"Why don't you lay the bed back and take a nap?" I suggested.

"That sounds really good, actually," she said, lifting up the remote for the bed.

"You did a good job, Mama, now you need to rest. I have a feeling this little girl's gonna keep you on your toes."

"Don't I know it."

I left her alone so she could try and sleep and went to get a closer look at Charlie.

"She's beautiful," I whispered to Jason.

He tore his gaze away from his daughters and looked at me with tears in his eyes.

"I'm the luckiest man alive."

Chapter Eleven

I woke up feeling excited and optimistic about the coming day.

Not only did Amy May have a healthy, beautiful, baby girl, but today Carmen and I would be reporting for duty in our new office.

I wasn't normally a morning person necessarily, but this morning I was practically bright eyed and bushy tailed ... in other words, I was like Carmen was every day.

I got up early, made everyone breakfast, and kissed Cade before heading out the door.

The kiss had actually gotten away from me for a minute, and I'd been seconds away from putting my hand down his pants, but I refocused and remembered that I wanted to stop and get some cupcakes on the way so Carmen and I could celebrate and promised him I'd finish what I'd started that night after dinner.

"Call me later, darlin'," Cade murmured against my lips, causing a quiver to run down my spine.

"Will do," I replied, then sauntered out the door, putting an extra sway in my hips when I felt his eyes following me out.

"Keep it up and I'll spank that ass later," he growled from behind me.

I laughed and glanced over my shoulder at him. "Promises, promises."

Feeling giddy, I hopped in the Caravan and drove the short trip from my house to main street. After I'd parked in the parking space outside the office that had *my name on it*, I walked over to the bakery and opened the door with a smile.

"Good morning, beautiful people," I called happily, as the jingle sounded over my head announcing my entrance.

"Morning, Lila," Jordan, Amy May's right hand, replied. "You sure are chipper today."

"It's a beautiful day, Jordan. The sun is shining, Amy May had little Charlie, and I'm here to get celebratory cupcakes for the opening of my office."

"I stopped by and saw Amy May and Charlie last

night. She's absolutely adorable … It's a bit surprising she doesn't have a little weenus though," Jordan joked.

I laughed and said, "Little weenususes, or the lack thereof, are always surprising. But, yeah, total plot twist, right?"

"And I should tell you, your girl Carmen already came by and picked up celebratory cupcakes."

"God, I love that girl," I said, my heart warming over the fact that Carmen was as excited as I was. "In that case, I guess I'll grab a dozen assorted donuts. Looks like we're going into a sugar coma today."

"You got it," Jordan said, and went about boxing them up.

A few moments later I wished her a good day and set out to the office with my bakery box in hand.

Since I knew Carmen had beat me to work, I opened the door and let myself in, taking a deep breath of freshly painted, floral-perfumed air as I stepped inside.

"Aww, Carmen, you got cupcakes *and* flowers!"

Carmen turned from where she was placing a vase on the counter and said, "It's a big day."

"It is, and I'm so happy to share it with you. Here," I said, showing her my box. "More carbs and sugar to keep us going."

"*Oh my gosh*, I'm gonna have to do extra workouts

with Bran if we keep this up," Carmen said, patting her flat stomach.

"Ah," I started with a wave of my hand. "Tomorrow we'll have salads. It's all about balance."

"I put the cupcakes in the breakroom and saw all the drinks in the fridge."

"That was all Cade. He came by last night and stocked us up with drinks and snacks."

"What a sweetheart."

"That he is," I replied happily. "I'll just drop these donuts in there and then I'm going to sit in my new chair behind my new desk."

"Enjoy it. Oh, and we had a message this morning, so I called the woman back and she's coming in at ten this morning. Her son didn't come home last night, and she said her sister told her the cops can't do anything about it since he hasn't been gone long enough. But she's worried."

"Sounds good, thanks."

I turned on my Keurig and made myself a cup of coffee, chose a maple bar, and whistled my way down the hall to my office.

I busied myself with work until it was almost ten o'clock and then I started back out to the front to meet the new client.

"What's the client's name?" I asked, popping my head into Carmen's office on my way.

"Mrs. Schneider."

"Thanks," I said, then paused and asked, "Do you think we need to get a receptionist for the front?"

"Ohhhh, that would be fun. We would be totally legit," Carmen said gleefully.

"That's what I was thinking."

"You want me to do a writeup and post the job opening?" she offered.

"Yeah, that would be great. Thanks."

"No problem."

I walked into the reception area just as the door open and a frazzled-looking woman came walking in.

"Mrs. Wilkes," she asked, and I felt a thrill run through me at sound of my new last name.

"Yes, and you're Mrs. Schneider?" I confirmed, holding out my hand to her.

She shook it lightly and said, "Yes."

"Can I get you anything? Water? Coffee?" I offered.

"No, thank you."

"Why don't we sit," I said, gesturing to the two high-back chairs that were angled toward each other.

She looked so harried that I figured she'd be more comfortable in the casual setting rather than in my office sitting in front of my desk.

I grabbed a notepad and pen off of the back side of the counter and joined her.

"Carmen, my associate, mentioned that your son is missing," I prompted.

"Yes," Mrs. Schneider began, wringing her hands together in her lap. "Cliff is very social and goes out a lot – he's a senior in high school – but he always comes home. *Always*. But last night, he didn't, and when I woke up this morning to find him still gone, I checked my phone, but there were no messages. I've tried calling and texting, and have called some of his friends, but no one knows where he is."

"Can I get the names of his friends, and girlfriends if you know them, and a photo. Does he have a job?" I asked.

"No, he's been focusing on football and keeping his grades up so he can graduate. I always told him he'll have time enough to work, that once you start working you don't really stop, and he should enjoy this time in his life." She reached into her purse and pulled out her wallet, then handed me a photo. "I know we all have pictures on our phones now adays, but I still like to get them printed so I can carry him around with me, you know? This is from one of his games."

I accepted the photo and was only mildly surprised to see a face I'd recognized.

"Ma'am," I began, gentling my voice. "I'm not sure how much you know, but Cliff was involved romantically with one of his teachers. I learned this through another case I was working on and gave the information to the police. His disappearance may be related to that relationship."

Mrs. Schneider bent her head and began crying softly.

"Don't worry. I'll find him."

Chapter Twelve

"Thanks for meeting me, Bea, I know you have a lot going on," I told my friend as she sat across from me.

We were at Jake's again, which was now only a short walk from my office, but instead of having cake for lunch, I'd opted for a burger and fries. I hated to admit it, but I may have gone overboard on the sweets today.

"Yeah, no problem. I wanted to touch base with you, too."

"I ordered your soup for you. Are you sure you don't want more than that to eat?" I asked, furrowing my brow as I took in her pale skin. "You look like you're losing weight, and you didn't have much on you to begin with."

Bea was petite and small, with short hair that only furthered the pixie look she had going on.

"The soup's fine, I haven't really had much of an appetite lately."

"Is it really all because of work, or is there something else going on?" I prodded, reaching over to place my hand over hers. "You know you can tell me anything."

Bea let out a soft sigh and her eyes began to fill, which really freaked me out because Bea was the toughest chick I knew, and she never cried.

"Things are ... tough," she managed.

"With work? At home?"

She took a deep breath and met my eyes as she replied, "Both."

"What's happened?"

"You know we've had a couple adoption prospects fall through." I nodded. "Over the last few months, it's started to put a strain on me and Shannon and our relationship. We've been fighting a lot and, I don't know. Things aren't good. We've decided to put a pause on the adoption for now."

"Oh, Bea, I'm so sorry. But you and Shannon love each other. You're both so strong. I know you'll get through this."

She shrugged and said, "I don't know if we will, and me working all the time isn't helping, not that we really spend any time together when I'm not working. But between that and this case ... well, I'm not getting much sleep or really feeling all that hungry."

"Did it make things worse ... being there for Amy May?"

"It didn't help, but there was no way I was going to miss out on Amy May having baby Charlie just because it made things difficult for me and Shannon. We love her. We wouldn't do that."

"She loves you, too, which is why she'd understand."

"Here you go," our server said, and Bea quickly moved her hand off the table and sat back in her seat. "Broccoli cheddar soup for you and a burger with the works and fries. Can I get you anything else?"

"No, thanks," I said, glancing at Bea. And I could tell from the way she was stiffly sitting and the look on her face, that she was done talking about this.

She pulled her bowl closer to her and picked up the soup spoon. "What was this new case you wanted to discuss?"

I sighed, knowing if Bea was done talking, there was nothing I could do to pull more out of her. The woman was stubborn and didn't like talking about her private life on a good day. Let alone sharing her feelings. I was lucky to have gotten out of her what I did.

I told her about Mrs. Schneider and Cliff not coming home last night.

"The teacher has gone underground as well," Bea said, her voice strong and authoritative now that she was in cop mode. "After you told me what you'd found, I went to the husband, who said he'd kicked her out of the house and was filing for divorce. Then I went to the school, and they said she stopped showing up for work. We've had a BOLO out on her for a week, but nothing yet."

"So, it's possible Cliff decided to join her," I mused.

"Yeah, I'd say so. Why didn't the mom contact the department?"

"She said it was because he only didn't show last night and it hasn't been twenty-four hours yet," I explained.

Bea shook her head and said, "There is no rule about how long you have to wait to file a missing person's report. That's something made up for TV and movie drama and now it's a common misconception. Give me her information and I'll write it up when I get back."

"I'll text it to you when I get back to the office."

"Perfect."

I dipped my fry in the honey mustard I'd ordered on the side and added, "I have a meeting scheduled with all three of the women whose cars were jacked over the next few days. I went over your notes, of course, but I want to try and get a feel for it myself as well."

"Good. Let me know if you learn anything new."

"Of course I will. You gotta come over and see the new office."

"Yeah, I'm, uh, sorry I didn't come to help on move-in day."

"Don't worry about it," I told her. "We hired movers, and you know how Carmen is about putting stuff away and organizing."

Bea nodded. "And did I hear Cade's parents say they're moving here? I was surprised to see them at the hospital."

"Yup. They're planning to get a house here and split their time between here and Hawaii. Now that Alani is here and Cade and I are married, they want to be here with us."

"That's understandable. You good with it?"

I gave a half shrug and said, "Yeah, sure. They're the best and Elin and Lena love spending time with them. They've never really had grandparents in their lives, you know?"

"I do. And it helps that you all get along. I've never had that with Shannon's parents."

Shannon's parents hadn't adjusted well to Shannon coming out to them and had not been in favor of her marrying Bea.

"It does."

"Anyway, I hate to eat and run, but I'd better get back to the precinct."

"Okay, and, Bea, let's go out soon. Either the two of us, or we can organize a girls' night out."

She nodded and said, "Thanks, Lila."

"Anytime, babe."

Chapter Thirteen

"I don't want to talk to you," Alani called over her shoulder as she stormed into our house.

Rufus and C.B. jumped up and ran toward her, both vying for her attention as she walked past them.

"Calm down, Keiki, there's no reason to be upset," Cade's mom said as she and Cade's dad came in behind Alani.

They were all coming over this morning for brunch with Lena and Elin, who were going to be leaving us for a week. Eric, my ex and their father, was having a destination wedding and the twins were joining him and Mary in Anguilla. They were super excited about the trip, and I couldn't blame them. Luckily, Mary was a sweet woman who got along great with my kids.

"What's going on?" Cade asked his family, who were still squabbling.

"I walked in on them having *sex*," Alani said, spitting out the word like it was poison.

I covered my mouth with my hand so she wouldn't see me smiling.

"Keiki, it's normal for a husband and wife to make love," her mom told her.

Alani didn't look at her but kept her eyes on her brother. "In the living room."

"Pops, what are you thinking? You know Alani's there too," Cade admonished.

His dad simply shrugged, but his mom said, "It was early in the morning, Hiapo, you know your sister usually sleeps in."

"Oh, so it's my fault for getting up early and wanting a cup of coffee?" Alani asked, throwing her hands up in exasperation. "Why can't you do that stuff in your own bedroom instead riding him on the couch."

"*Hey!*" Cade's parents protested in unison.

"*Ah*, I didn't need to hear that," Cade complained.

"Yeah, well, I didn't need to *see* that," Alani retorted. "And now I can never *un*see it."

Unable to hold it in anymore, I burst out laughing.

"*Lila*," Cade warned, but there was no use. I'd caught the kind of giggles that keep going and going until your side hurts and tears are leaking out of the corners of your eyes.

I'd suffered plenty of humiliation in front of his family when we were in Hawaii, and it was nice to finally be on the other side of it.

"Sorry," I hiccupped, hugging my waist as I bent over and tried to stop.

"What's so funny?" Lena asked as she and Elin walked into the living room rolling their suitcases behind them.

"*Nothing*," everyone but me cried.

I finally got myself under control while they all said their hellos.

"You good?" Cade asked, a small smile playing on his lips.

I looked up at him and wiped my eyes with the back of my hand. "Yeah, I am. Wow, I haven't laughed like that in a long time."

"I love seeing you laugh, I just wish it was for a different reason," he said with a chuckle.

I grinned at him and pulled him down for a kiss. "Sorry, babe. I'll go get food started."

I was in the kitchen pulling out bacon and eggs when my phone rang, and I saw it was Carmen.

"Hey, Carmen, what's up?" I asked when I answered.

"Hiya. I know you guys are doing the big breakfast send-off for Lena and Elin, so I'll be quick. Just wanted to let you know I found Cliff and that nasty teacher of his, and both Bea and Mrs. Schneider have been notified."

I'd asked her to take over the case since I needed to make sure the kids were ready for their trip.

"That's awesome. You're the best, Carmen."

"Aww, thanks. Now you go have fun with the family and give the twins a kiss from me. Bran's making me go with him on a ten-mile bike ride, so you may never see me again."

I chuckled and said, "Be safe and tell Bran hello from me."

"Will do. Toodles!"

"Lila, sweetie, let me help," Ma said as she joined me in the kitchen.

She was a much better cook than I'd ever be, so I said, "Happily."

Usually, Alani joined us when we were preparing food, but this time she kept her distance, which I found completely understandable. Just thinking of it had me smiling again as I whisked eggs.

"That baby Charlie is just the sweetest," Ma said suddenly.

I glanced warily at her and agreed, "She sure is."

"It must be nice, having a baby in the house."

Oh, Lord. Here we go.

"*Mm-hm,*" I muttered noncommittally.

"You know, you're not getting any younger, and I know Cade would love to see you ripe with his child."

That made me choke on my own spit.

"Jeez, Ma," I managed once I stopped choking.

"What? I'm just saying … I'd love a little baby to spoil."

"You can spoil Charlie, or Elin and Lena. Excuse me a minute," I said, leaving the bowl of beaten eggs and hurrying out of the room, where I ended up crashing into Cade's massive body.

"Hey," he said, grasping my shoulders to steady me. "You okay?"

"Yeah, your mom's just starting with the baby stuff … I needed a minute."

He grinned and tucked my unruly curls behind my ear.

"She means well."

"I know, which is why I walked away rather than losing my cool."

"I was coming to tell you I just got off the phone with Slade and I'm gonna need to go to the compound after breakfast."

His tone had my stomach clenching.

"Is something wrong?"

"The Diablos are acting up."

I knew he wouldn't tell me anything else, club business was between club members and that was that, but the name said enough.

The Diablos Rebeldes were another motorcycle club and bad dudes. Before our wedding Cade had been doing some recon for his club and I'd mistakenly thought he'd been abducted by the Diablos and may have accidentally put myself, Carmen, and Bran in danger. It had all worked out okay, and Cade had saved the day, but I'd spent the last few months worrying there'd be blow back on Cade's club because of it.

They'd been quiet up 'til now.

Chapter Fourteen

The house was eerily quiet.

Eric and Mary had picked up the kids and they were off for their vacation. Alani, Ma, and Pops had gone back to the cabin and had asked to take the dogs with them so they could run around. And Cade still hadn't come back from the compound.

I'd gone into the twins' rooms and did a quick cleaning, which is something I did every time they went to their dad's or on a trip. I liked being in their space, it made me feel closer to them somehow, and I wanted them to come home to a nice, organized room.

With that done and the rest of the house good since everyone had pitched in on cleanup after breakfast, I poured myself a glass of wine and went out onto the screened-in back patio.

This is where my office had been up until recently, and we hadn't had time to do anything to the space yet. So, all that was there was an old wicker rocking loveseat and a planter I used as an end table.

I sat down and rocked, enjoying the night sounds as I visualized what I wanted to do with the space.

We could get new patio furniture and make it a fun indoor/outdoor space with a bar. Or we could make it into a game room ... put in a ping pong table, maybe some arcade-style games. *Or we could close it in and make it a nursery.*

Where had that thought come from?

I locked the thought down and looked around as if afraid I'd said it aloud and made it true.

I took a gulp of wine.

Do I want that? To have a baby? The twins are twelve and it would be like starting all over again ... But a baby with Cade could be a beautiful thing...

I shook my head and took out my phone.

Once I dialed the number, I put the phone to my ear and listened to it ring.

"Hello?"

"Hey, Amy May, I didn't wake anyone, did I?"

"No," she replied with a laugh. "There's not a lot of sleeping happening over here. Isn't that right, Miss Charlie?"

"I figured."

"What's up? Are you all right?" she asked.

"Yeah, it's good. The kids left today for Eric's wedding and Cade's got club business and I'm just sitting out back having a glass of wine. I thought of you and wanted to hear your voice."

"I forgot that was today. Are they excited for the trip?"

"They are. Lena's excited for the surfing and Elin wants to do a tour of the island."

"And you? Are you okay with Eric marrying Mary?" she asked. Amy May had been my best friend forever and she and Jason used to hang out with me and Eric all the time. They'd never been super close, but she was there for the good and bad times of my previous marriage.

"Yeah, sure. I think she's good for him and they're both great with the kids. I'm happy that he's happy."

I wanted to tell Amy May about the Diablos, but I didn't want to worry her. She'd helped me and Carmen out by researching and finding information on the Diablos when I was looking for Cade, so she knew the history, but with her just having Charlie and needing to rest, I didn't think I should bring it up.

"I was talking with Bea, and we agreed when you're up for it, a girls' night is long overdue."

Amy May groaned and said, "God, yes! I need a night out with you guys so badly. Although, I had a little glass of wine with dinner – I pumped and dumped – and was pretty buzzed. I'm a cheap date."

"That's the best kind," I joked.

"No doubt."

"I don't want to keep you, I just wanted to check in and see how you guys are doing."

"Tired, but good."

"I bet. Let me know if you need anything."

"I will. And if you get time this week, stop by. We'd love to see you," Amy May said.

"I'll do that. Get some sleep."

"Good night, Lila. Thanks for calling."

I disconnected and put my phone on the seat beside me then settled back and sipped on my wine as a million thoughts seemed to crowd my mind.

Right as I'd decided relaxing wasn't working and I should just go to bed, my phone rang.

It was Bea.

"Hey, everything okay?" I asked, getting out of the loveseat and walking back inside.

"We got another one," she said.

Not quite following, I asked, "Another what?" with my mind on her and Shannon.

I'd been worrying about them after our lunch and

hoped she was calling me about my offer to be there if she needed to talk.

"Another GPS victim. I'm heading into the station now."

Bea must have put the phone down because her voice was muffled when she said, "It's my job, Shannon. You know that. I can't just leave it for someone else to handle. It's important."

I thought I heard Shannon retort, *"Yeah, your job is always what's important,"* and I winced.

I hated that my friends were fighting.

"You there?" she asked, her voice loud and clear so I knew she was talking to me.

"Yeah, do you want me to meet you there?"

"Yes. Please."

"Okay, I'll see you in ten."

Chapter Fifteen

After shooting off a text to Cade letting him know I was meeting Bea, I headed into town to the police precinct.

I'd been there plenty of times over the years, since Bea and I became friends, so everyone knew me, and I knew them. I also knew the coffee was terrible. Often so strong from sitting forever and constantly being reheated, that you could smell it as soon as you stepped foot in the door.

"Hey, Tash," I called to the woman running dispatch as I walked back toward Bea's desk.

"Hey, girl," she replied.

Bea had beat me there. She was running her hands through her hair, which had grown out from its usual pixie cut to a bob. She'd thrown on her uniform, but her face was free from makeup, as if she'd already been getting ready for bed when she got the call.

My heart ached at the expression on her face, and I wished there was something I could do for her but knew the best thing to do was simply *be there*.

"Bea," I called, causing her head to swing toward me.

"Thanks for coming, I know you've got your hands full."

"Actually, I don't. The kids are off with Eric for his wedding trip and Cade is working, so I'm all yours."

Her face fell and she rubbed her eyes with her fists.

"How did I not realize it was already time for Eric's wedding? Jesus, Lila, I'm a shit friend."

"Bea, no," I said, placing my hand on her shoulder. I wanted to pull her in for a hug but knew she wouldn't want me to in her place of work while she was in uniform. "You're the best. It's okay to focus on what's going on in your own life. Eric's wedding isn't a big deal, and neither is my moving furniture into my office. The kids will be back, and the office will still be there when you have the time. Don't add more stress to yourself, okay. Not over me."

She nodded and patted my hand gently.

"The latest victim is in the conference room. I wanted to wait for you so she can tell her story one time and be on her way."

"Great, let's do it."

We moved down the row of desks to the conference room, where a pretty woman with dark skin and braids sat, her hands wrapped around an untouched mug of coffee.

Smart lady.

"Mrs. Boyd, sorry to keep you waiting," Bea said as we stepped inside and sat at the table.

"It's okay. I've just been going over it all in my mind," Mrs. Boyd said with a sigh. "It's really the craziest thing."

"What do you mean?" Bea asked as she flipped open her notebook.

"Well ... I knew where I was going. Using the GPS is more of a habit, a crutch. Even if I know how to get someplace, I still use the GPS on my phone just in case there's traffic and I need to be rerouted, or if I get caught up in a podcast and miss a turn. So, it started taking me a different direction, nowhere near where I was going, and seconds after I realized it and was about to turn around, I ran something over and blew a tire."

"You felt it? That you ran over something?" Bea asked, and I knew this was a new bit of information.

She nodded. "I did, and I had to get control of the car before I swerved off the road. I was able to pull off to the side and got out to check the tire. As I rounded the car, I looked back, and I swear I saw some sort of sharp contraption in the road, like it was done on purpose, and as I turned to look at the tire, I heard something behind me and then felt a pinch in my neck. The next thing I knew I was being woken up by a nurse outside the hospital in Greenswood."

"Do you remember where you were when it happened?"

"I think about twenty miles north of Greenswood. I was heading to this boutique off the 24 but was way east of it. I live in the Heights and go out that way a lot but can't pinpoint exactly where I was because there was nothing around but trees."

"What were you driving?" I asked, mentally comparing what she said to what the other three carjacking victims had said.

"A Mercedes. G-Wagon, uh, G-Class."

"And you felt a pinch at your neck, like they injected you with something," Bea confirmed.

"Yes. And the doctor at the hospital confirmed it. They couldn't tell what it was, because whatever it was had already been absorbed or something, but they found the puncture mark in my neck."

"Look, I realize that you may never be able to find my vehicle, because they're probably breaking it down and selling parts or filing off the VIN number selling the whole car, but this can't keep happening. I just hope you catch whoever's doing this so we can get justice and stop them from doing this to someone else."

"We're doing our very best, I promise you. In the meantime, I'll get your report written up and get you a copy for your insurance company," Bea said.

"Thank you. Can you email it to me? My husband should be waiting, and I'd like to go home now."

"Of course. I'll walk you out."

While Bea was doing that, I went through my own notes and compared each of the victims' statements.

Bea walked back in a few moments later and said, "Well, her seeing the device they used to flatten the tire is new, and the fact that they somehow hacked into her GPS to change the direction she was going without her being aware of it, are both new discoveries."

"Yeah, so you know what this means," I began, and at the same time I said, "I need to go undercover," Bea said, "We need to find someone who knows about hacking into phones or GPS." Her eyes flew to me when what I'd said registered, and she said, "No, Lila. Absolutely not."

Chapter Sixteen

"Thanks so much for coming along," Cade's mom said as we pulled up in front of a prospective house. "This is the one I like, but your Pops said I should have you look it over to make sure there's no underlying issues."

"That's what the home inspection's for, Ma," Cade replied. "But I'm happy to do a precheck. Anything you need."

Staci with an I was waiting for us on the porch, and, no, I didn't miss the way her eyes automatically moved to Cade. By the time we reached her to say hello, her cheeks were pink and rosy, so when it came time for me to shake her hand, I made sure she noticed the stank eye I was throwing her way.

She had the grace to look embarrassed before she focused on Ma and led us inside.

The house was closer to Cade's cabin than our house and was on a couple acres of land. It was two-bedroom ranch, with a basement, and a big wraparound porch.

Cade left us to do his inspection, while his mom took me back outside.

"This is my favorite part," she said as we walked around the porch to the back, which overlooked a wooded lot with a stream running through it. "You know we have to live near some type of water."

Their home in Hawaii was right on the ocean and had the most amazing views.

"It's lovely," I agreed. "Very peaceful."

I imagined Rufus and C.B. running in and out of the water, which made me realize, "Hey, what about Boone?"

Boone was their beagle.

"Oh, you know Boone, he's a ramblin' man. Susie and the rest of the neighbors will see that he's fed. We talked about moving him out here with us, but all the back and forth would be too much for him. He's an island dog at heart."

I didn't blame him.

We walked around the property for a bit, then she

took me up the steps to the back entrance, which opened up into the kitchen.

"And this is my second favorite part."

"Oh, this is beautiful," I gushed as I took in the kitchen.

There was plenty of counter with cabinet space underneath ... it almost took up all of the walls in the room, save the section with the stove and refrigerator. And above the counters were floating shelves. Finally, in the far corner there was a built-in bench with cushions topping it.

"Isn't it great?" she asked with a smile. "I'll probably want to put in some sort of island just for more seating and a place to do my prepping and chopping, but other than that, it's pretty perfect."

It was a chef's kitchen, and she would actually use it the way it was meant to be used.

"It really is."

She showed me the rest of the house and we eventually met up with Cade and Staci ... hmmm ... in the garage, where he was looking at the water heater and she was looking at his ass.

It looks like me and Staci are about to have problems.

Before I could say anything, she looked up and hurried over to us, her cheeks once again pink.

"Sorry, sorry!" she exclaimed, and since Ma didn't

ask why Staci was apologizing, I figured she'd seen the same thing I had.

"If you want my commission, Ms. Staci, you'll keep it in your pants," Ma said.

I could stop the snicker ... *Yup, she saw it.*

"I apologize," Staci said again. "Why don't I let you all look your fill and I'll wait outside."

"I think that's best," Ma replied.

As Staci scurried out, I turned to my mother-in-law and threw my arms around her neck. "I love you."

"*Oh*," she said, and I could hear the emotion in her voice. "I love you too, Keiki."

My heart swelled at her use of the term of endearment she always used for Alani.

"You guys good?" Cade asked from behind us.

We broke apart and I tried to casually wipe my cheeks.

"Yeah, how about you?" I asked.

He gave me a confused look, then said, "Everything looks good to me, Ma. Well-kept and updated. You may have to look at getting a new air-conditioning unit in a couple years, but the inspection will give you more info on that, and maybe it's under warranty."

"Thanks, Hiapo. Now, how about I take you out for a treat for helping me out?"

"Cupcakes?" I asked hopefully.

She chuckled and said, "Sure," bringing a hand up to pat my cheek affectionately.

We took Cade's truck into town and stopped at Cynthia's Coffee and Books, since we knew she'd have Amy May's delicacies in stock, and Cade could get the coffee he liked from there.

Once we were inside, Cade's mom immediately got distracted by the latest Nora Roberts book, while Cade and I made our way to the little café area in the back of the shop. We passed a couple of sitting areas with lush chairs, and the stage where she held everything from poetry readings to acoustic jam sessions.

"There's my favorite newlyweds," Cynthia said when she caught sight of us.

"Hey, Cynthia, how's business?" I asked, giving her a hug.

"I can't complain," she replied, offering her cheek to Cade, who complied by kissing it briefly. "What can I get you other than coffee?"

I had free coffee for life for finding and bringing back her stolen books, and once I'd gotten married, she'd extended the perk to Cade. We always made sure to leave extra in the tip jar to make up for it.

"Your biggest cupcake. I don't even care what flavor it is. Surprise me," I replied.

"Just coffee for me, thanks," Cade added.

"You got it. Why don't you make yourselves comfortable and I'll bring it over?"

We found a free loveseat and settled into it, Cade's arm coming around my shoulders to pull me in close.

"I feel like we haven't gotten to spend any time together, which is crazy since the kids are gone," I murmured.

"Yeah, things have been hectic with my parents deciding to move and things heating up with the Diablos. I hate that by the time I get home you're already asleep."

"You know I don't mind if you wake me up," I said, tilting my head back to look up at him.

His grin was sexy as hell when he asked, "Yeah?"

"You know it."

He snuggled me closer and said, "I know. I just feel bad because you need your sleep. You've been working a lot of hours too."

"I would rather be woken up by you than sleep. I promise."

I felt his chuckle rumble in his chest. "I'll keep that in mind next time."

"You do that ... and I still need to fill you in on this new case with Bea and the department."

"I need to give you a head's up about this shit with the Diablos, too."

"What do you say we go out tonight, have some dinner, and catch up?" I suggested.

"I say, why don't we stay *in* tonight, have some dinner, and catch up?"

"Mmmm. Yours is better."

Chapter Seventeen

Unfortunately, Cade got called back to the compound, so there was no dinner or catchup.

Instead, I called Carmen and Bea and invited them over for pizza and wine to discuss next steps for the carjacking case.

I put on some Fleetwood Mac and tidied up while I waited for my friends, and the pizza to arrive. And needing to feel their presence, I stepped into each of the twins' rooms for a few moments.

I was no stranger to them being gone while they split time between me and their dad, but it never got any easier.

When I heard the front door open, I ran to the living room, excited to no longer be alone.

"I never realized how much I need to be around people until this week," I said with a chuckle as I turned the corner to see Bea standing at the door with a frown. "What?"

"You left your door unlocked again, Lila," she replied sternly.

Both she and Cade were always on me for not taking security seriously enough.

"I knew you and Carmen were on the way, so I left it unlocked," I argued, even though that was a lie. I pretty much left it unlocked until I went to bed at night.

Bea gave me a look that let me know she did *not* believe me.

"Oh, you brought wine," I said, hoping the subject change would work.

Bea passed me and headed toward the kitchen, calling back, "Yeah, I figured the more the merrier."

"That's my motto," I quipped.

She went straight for the end drawer and pulled out my wine opener.

O-kay, guess she's not wasting any time.

Taking her cue, I moved to the cupboard behind her and pulled down three wine glasses.

"I've got white in the fridge as well," I told her.

"I'm good with this," she said as she turned the corkscrew.

"Lila, you've gotta start locking up," Carmen called before I heard the door close behind her.

Great, now she's getting in on it too.

I ignored Bea's pointed look and called back, "White or red?"

"White, please," Carmen said with an easy smile as she joined us in the kitchen. "Hey, Bea," she said, moving to give Bea, and then me, a hug.

"How's it going?" Bea asked her.

"Can't complain," Carmen replied. "You?"

"Oh, I can, and will, complain," Bea retorted dryly.

I gave Carmen a *"yikes"* look, then grabbed the white wine out of the refrigerator and poured her some.

Bea tilted the red wine bottle at me in question and I nodded in response.

Once we all had our glasses, I asked, "Do you guys want to go sit out back or go into the living room?"

"Back," they said in unison, making Carmen giggle.

Because of my inability to lock the front door and other security-related negligence on my part, Cade had installed a whole mess of cameras around the house, including one of those doorbell things. So, when the pizza delivery arrived, I'd be notified by a little chime that he's on the porch.

We settled around the table outside and jumped right in.

"Going back to what you said the other night, Lila, I want to urge you *not* to try and go undercover to find these car jackers by yourself," Bea said, taking a big gulp of wine.

Carmen and I glanced at each other, which made Bea sigh.

"And even as I'm saying this, I realize historically, no matter what I say, you usually go off half-cocked and do whatever you want anyway. Whether we're talking about trying to solve a murder case, a human trafficking case, drugs, or the disappearance of *your man*." The last she said with air quotes.

"Guilty on all counts," I replied, and Carmen snickered.

Bea shot Carmen a look that had her biting her lower lip, then glared at me. "Lila, you know it's only because I love you and want to do my best to keep you out of harm's way, even though you seem bound and determined to always land right in it, that I tell you not to do these things and to let my department handle it."

I held up my hand and pointed out, "This time you brought me in."

"Yeah, but not to use you as bait. Just to get your help in trying to figure out what the hell is going on."

She cleared her throat and I swear I could hear her mentally counting to ten.

I often brought out this reaction in people.

"That being said ... I know even without my blessing, not only will you do it anyway, but you'll find a way to get all of our friends involved. I know you don't mean to, but it usually happens. So, I'm going to agree to help set you up to go undercover, but with conditions."

I clapped my hands together and let out a little squeal just as my phone notified me that the pizza had arrived.

"Hold that thought," I said, standing quickly. "Provisions have arrived."

I went to grab the two large pizzas, breadsticks, and brownie pie – *don't judge* – and hurried back to my friends.

"Wow, is that all for us?" Carmen asked, and I knew she was already dreading Bran's workout the next morning.

"If we have any leftovers, Cade will eat it."

"Are you planning to just eat it out of the box?" Bea asked, and when my face clearly said *I had been*, she got up and went inside to get plates and napkins.

I grabbed a slice of spinach, feta, and black olive thin crust and groaned when the flavors hit my tongue.

"Is that good?" Carmen asked, scrunching up her nose.

"The other one is a meat-lovers and there's garlic knots."

"Yummmmm."

"Here you go," Bea said, passing us each a plate and a napkin and then putting more napkins in the center of the table.

"Thanks," Carmen said, placing the plate squarely in front of her and folding the napkin into a triangle before picking up another one and placing it on her lap.

"Okay, so ... conditions?" I prodded once Bea had made her plate.

"You'll wear a wire. You won't make any moves without discussing them with me first. Our friends stay out of it." When Carmen opened her mouth to protest, Bea pointed a finger at her and shook her head. "And finally, you don't put yourself in unnecessary danger. If you run into trouble, you notify me and wait for back up."

I started to protest, but Bea pointed that finger my way and said, "These are nonnegotiable."

"Fine," I said, the word coming out like a whine. "But there's no way that any car jacker is going to want the Caravan, or anything the precinct has to offer, so I'm gonna need to rent a car. Something expensive and flashy."

"Aww, are you sure I can't ride shotgun?" Carmen begged.

"No," Bea and I said together.

Bea was right about one thing. I didn't want to endanger any of my friends again, and even though Carmen worked with me and that came with some danger, I had a feeling this was going to be something I didn't want her involved in.

Chapter Eighteen

I woke up slowly, my mind foggy from wine and sleep, and felt Cade's lips on my neck. When his tongue entered the game, my body fully awoke, instantly needy and wanting.

Laying on my side, I reached behind me and curled my fingers in his hair as his hand made its way under my sleep tank to cup my breast. His hand was so big that he palmed me easily, and when he brushed his thumb over my taut nipple, my body shivered.

"You said to wake you…" his voice was deep and husky, and I felt the heat of his breath caress my ear.

I moved my hand to cover his and urged it down, over my belly, and into my shorts.

Understanding my request, his fingers caressed my soft folds as I bucked against them. Knowing my body as well as his own, he worked me over quickly and easily, until I was panting and writhing in ecstasy.

Cade pushed my shorts down, removing the barrier between us, then lifted and positioned my legs until he could slide easily inside of me.

What started sleepy and sweet quickly escalated into frenzied and desperate.

I moved my hand so I could awkwardly clutch the side of his ass as he pounded into me, grasping the sheet beneath us with my free hand. I moved back, meeting his thrusts easily, as he began to work my clit once more.

"*Jesus, Cade*," I cried, adjusting my position to give him access to go deeper.

"*Fuck*, babe."

As we came down off the high, I shifted to turn and snuggle into him.

"*Oh, shit*," I said with a laugh.

"What?" he asked roughly.

"I forgot ... Bea slept over. She's in Lena's room."

Cade chuckled and said, "Well, I hope she's a heavy sleeper, 'cause we were *not* quiet."

I ducked my head against his chest.

"Did you guys drink too much?" he asked, running has hand over my hair.

"No," I began with a sigh. "She and Shannon are having problems. Because the adoption journey has been difficult ... they've been fighting. And they usually never fight. I wish I could help."

"You know, darlin', all you can do is be there for them, as support. You can't fix their problems, and they probably wouldn't thank you for trying."

"I know. I just hate that they're going through this. They've always been this great, happy, stable couple, you know? Like the gold standard."

"Well, that's hard for anyone to maintain," Cade said. "They're just human, like everyone else. And they'll figure it out. One way or another."

"I hope it's one way ... or is it another?" I asked, furrowing my brow as I leaned back to catch his eye. "Which one is the one where they stay together, and everything works out?"

Cade grinned and me and simply said, "I hope they work it out too."

We were quiet for a few moments, and my mind drifted to the twins.

"Hey," I said softly.

"Yeah?"

"As much as it pains me to say it, thanks for getting Elin and Lena the phones for their birthday. It's been great being able to shoot them a text just to say what's up or ask how their doing."

I felt his chest shake with laughter beneath my

cheek.

"Elin doesn't say much, just 'it's good,' or 'Love you, too,' but Elena's been sending pictures and videos. It makes them being gone not so terrible."

"You're welcome. They've been texting me too. Did you see the one of Lena with the surfboard?"

"Yeah. She looked happy," I murmured, thinking how fast they were growing up.

"How's everything at the new place?" he asked.

"Really good. I think I'm going to hire a receptionist. It would really help free Carmen and I up to work on our cases and focus on field work."

"Sounds like a plan."

"Carmen has the job description all typed up and is waiting for the word from me and she'll post it on job sites."

"I bet she is," he mused, his tone laced with humor.

"Hiring her was the best decision I've made. Hopefully we'll have the same kind of luck with a receptionist."

"You will. You know what works and what doesn't."

I smiled, loving his faith in me. It was strange having someone who understood me so well, who had my back no matter what, and was always my biggest cheerleader. My marriage with Eric hadn't been terrible, at least not until he stepped out on me with Shirly Finkle, but our relationship had never been like that. The focus had always been on him and building *his* career.

"You're the best thing that ever happened to me, you know that?" I asked, moving up his body so I was above him and our mouths were aligned.

"Ditto," he said with a grin, his teeth glowing in the dark room.

I brushed my lips against him, loving the soft feel of his own, before he opened beneath me, and I swept inside.

God, I'll never get tired of the taste of him.

That fire lit once more, but this time our lovemaking was less frantic, as I took the wheel.

Before I fell asleep, content and satiated in his arms, I murmured, "Thanks for waking me up."

Chapter Nineteen

"This is the most beautiful car I have ever sat my butt in," I cooed, wiggling said butt in the plush seat as I ran my hand lovingly over the dash.

It was a cherry-red Jaguar F-Type, which I wouldn't have been able to identify before Bea pulled it into the lot and told me what it was. But she was a beauty.

"She's also the most expensive, so please, for the love of God, be careful. It's used, but still costs probably triple what your Caravan does, okay?" Bea asked, and I could see the worry in her eyes.

Not just over the car but for my safety.

"I promise I won't do anything crazier than knowingly drive this high-class car into a known car-jacking, wearing a wire, and trying to bust up some bad guys," I promised, crossing my heart dramatically.

Bea let out a low growl.

"We good?" I asked her.

"I'm having second, no triple, thoughts about this."

"Don't worry, Bea. Once we get the guys on tape, I snap some pictures of them, and I let you know my location, this case will be over."

"I know. You're right. Let's just go over everything *one more time...* You drive in the same direction as the victims, and we'll be following close behind. You know to expect the sharp object on the road, so watch for it and avoid it, then pull over. Leave your phone on and on the seat so I can track your location. You lock your doors, stay in the car, and snap photos with your camera. Do not get out of the car. The wire is there to record any conversation that may occur. Don't do anything reckless; just wait for us to arrive."

Once she'd double checked my wire, the location in the GPS, and paced back and forth a few more times, we agreed it was time for me to get on the road.

Realizing I'd still never been able to tell Cade about this case and fill him in on the plan, I shot him a quick text before getting my head in the game and taking off.

Babe. I'm working on that case with Bea. I

still never got the chance to give you the low down but I'm safe & Bea has my back. I'll see you tonight. Hopefully we can finally have that dinner. Love you, Lila.

I started to put on a classic rock station, but then, thinking the person who drove this car would need something more sophisticated, I put on jazz instead.

By the time I was ten miles out from where I'd programmed into the map, I saw the directions change. It was only a second, and if I hadn't been looking for it, I would have missed it, but it did in fact change and I was no longer headed in the right direction.

Knowing Bea was listening, I said, "The GPS just changed. I'm off of the 15 passing Trailor Road."

I could imagine the victims had been watching the road, singing along with the radio, and completely trusting that they were going the right way. Why wouldn't they be? The fact that this was even happening was diabolical.

Aware and ready for the next step of the plan, I tried to be normal.

I kept my speed five above the limit, kept my eyes forward, and did my best to seem like I was completely innocent. But in reality, I was watching all of my mirrors, my peripheral vision, and was on the edge of my seat waiting for the shit to hit the fan.

There.

If I hadn't been paying attention, I never would have noticed the small row of spikes on the right shoulder of the road. They were sticking out just enough to get the right tire, but not so far out that it would be obvious to anyone driving by.

I swerved just enough to miss it, then pulled over to the side of the road as if I'd hit it.

I pressed Bea's number on my phone and placed it on the seat. She'd answer it and use it to get my location. Then I turned off the car and waited.

After a few moments, I realized there was no one around, at least not that I could see.

They probably didn't hear any kind of noise from the tire deflating, and I hadn't swerved or anything, so maybe they didn't know I was there. Or they know I didn't have a flat so they weren't going to come out of hiding to grab me or the car.

"I have to get out of the car and act like I just blew a tire," I said loudly, knowing Bea would be cursing me on her end.

I took the keys out of the ignition and put them in my pocket. Then I grabbed my camera and got out to play the confused victim.

"*Oh my!*" I cried as I slammed the car door. "I wonder what happened?"

Okay, so I'd never taken an acting class.

I glanced back as I rounded the car and noticed the sharp device was no longer there, then turned my head and looked down at my not-flat tire.

"*Oh, no ...* Guess I need to call triple A."

As soon as the words were out of my mouth, I not only heard the soft crunch of a footstep behind me, but I *felt* the body closing in and spun around quickly, doing a squat as I did so I didn't inadvertently get a needle in the neck.

"What the?" a male voice said with a scowl. Then, "*You!*"

I looked up so quickly that I lost my balance and fell back. I moved my arms quickly and caught myself with my hands, but I felt the sting of the gravel beneath my palms.

"You've got to be kidding me," he said, and I had to agree with the sentiment.

It was Cueball. The ugly bastard who'd shoved my face in cake and kept my husband chained to his basement months prior.

I stood as he put his fingers in his mouth and let out a loud whistle.

More Diablos Rebeldes came out of the trees and joined us next to the Jag.

"What's this?" the one I remembered was called Scam asked.

"You remember this broad, doncha?" Cueball asked, waving the syringe in my face. "It's The Enforcer's old lady. The bitch who showed up with those two *Vineyard Vines* motherfuckers at the compound, when we had The Enforcer locked up."

"Oh yeah, she broke him out," Scam said.

"Who are you calling *The Enforcer*? Cade?" I asked. "I've never heard that one."

Although I have to admit, it fits.

"Why are you talking?" Cueball asked. *Rudely.* "Why are you even here? What the fuck is this?"

Crap, I had my camera hanging around my neck. I hadn't taken any pictures yet, but it didn't really matter... I had these guys' ugly mugs lasered in my brain.

"If she's The Enforcer's old lady, maybe she's here on his business?" another guy with an unfortunate mullet suggested.

"Drivin' a car like this? Like she knew what we was doin', got that camera, too. And look, her tire isn't flat. She's settin' us up ... *again*."

Cueball was looking mighty irritated, and I became very aware that there were six of them and one of me, and all I had on me were the car keys and a wire.

"Scam, tow the car as usual, but rather than dropping this one off at the hospital, we're taking her with us," Cueball decreed.

Great.

Chapter Twenty

There were a couple ways I could play this.

I could fight. Make them drag me kicking and screaming to the truck that had just miraculously pulled up. Which they would do, because, like I said, there were six of them and one of me. Six hulking, unattractive bikers.

Cade definitely beat this lot hands down, when it came to being a gorgeous, badass biker. These guys looked more like they were part of some reject club, where all the losers went when no one else would take them.

I probably shouldn't say that out loud.

I could run. But, as previously stated, six guys. Sure, I could probably outrun them in a footrace, but they had bikes and the truck, so...

I could play along. Go easily, no muss, no fuss, and bide my time until I found the perfect opening to fight or run.

Scam opened the passenger door and lifted up my purse. "You want this, Cue?"

"Nah, leave it with the car."

Shoot, I had my emergency Little Debbie cupcake in there, and I had a feeling I was gonna need it.

"You can't just leave my purse," I argued.

"Shut it!" Cueball shouted.

Jeez.

"There's something else, Cue. It looks like she's on a phone call with someone named Bea," Scam said, holding up my phone to show the profile photo of Bea I had programmed. She was in her uniform.

"Fuckin' hang it up, ya idiot," Cue snarled, as he turned to stalk toward me. "You on the phone with the cops?"

I decided it best to remain quiet.

Cueball stopped in front of me, put his hand on my shirt, and tore, causing the buttons to go flying and my shirt to fall open, revealing the wire taped to my stomach and chest.

Eyes wide, I tried to hold my shirt closed, but he reached out and tore the tape from my skin, pulling until he held the contraption in his hand.

"You're just full of surprises, aren't you? I should shoot you in the head and leave you on the side of the road."

I bit back a whimper, from his threat, and the stinging pain.

"You're lucky your old man's The Enforcer. Let's go."

He grabbed my arm hard enough that I knew there'd be a bruise and dragged me toward the waiting truck.

"You want me to bring the phone?" Scam called after us.

"Break it!" Cue yelled back. "Step on it until there's nothing left but dust."

He opened the door and moved to shove me inside, but of course the truck was raised, so I simply bent at the waist, hitting my diaphragm, and grunting loudly.

"Step up," Cue ordered. "And get in back."

"There's no room back there," I said, when I was up in the passenger seat.

"There should be a jump seat, and if not, sit on the floor."

I sat down on the floor, squeezed between the two bucket seats, and just knew I was getting grease and Lord knew what else on the seat of my jeans.

Cueball got into the driver's seat and started the truck.

When no one else got in and he started to pull away, I asked, "If no one else is riding with us, why do I have to sit on the floor?"

"Because that's where I throw all my trash."

"*Wow ... rude.*"

"I want you to put your head between your knees and shut your eyes. I don't need you seeing where I'm taking you, or anything like that. I'll let you know when you can get up."

"I can barely see over the dash like this–"

"Do it!" he yelled, and I quickly complied.

While we drove, I had time to go over Bea's conditions in my head. *Wear a wire, don't make any moves without discussing them with her first, keep our friends out of it, and don't put myself in unnecessary danger. If I do, wait for back up.*

Looked like I'd already failed four out of five. At least none of our friends were in this mess with me.

I thought about Cade, and how pissed he was going to be, and just hoped he didn't take it out on Bea. They didn't always see eye to eye, but one of the things they *did* agree with was keeping me out of dangerous situations. I didn't want him to blame her for bringing me in on this case.

Heck, I didn't want her to blame herself.

I was glad my kids were out of the country and safe

with their dad. I never wanted the possibility of my job touching their lives in a negative way. That's another reason I wanted to get an office outside of our home. For their safety.

"Are you almost there? I have to pee," I said, not lifting my head.

"God, do you ever shut up?" Cue asked.

"I've been quiet this whole time," I protested.

It was true, and it was also true that I really needed to use the restroom.

"Hold it. You got about ten more minutes."

"I don't know if I can," I admitted, hating the pitiful tone of my voice.

"Then piss yourself. Won't bother me."

"You're disgusting," I murmured against denim.

"I know you are but what am I?"

Jeez, it's like dealing with armed toddlers.

Chapter Twenty-One

The road we turned on was bumpy, rocky maybe, and took us about a mile down before the truck began to slow and eventually stop.

"Can I get up now?" I asked.

Cueball muttered under his breath but didn't answer.

I heard the door open and felt him get out but didn't move for fear of making him more annoyed.

Finally, the passenger door opened, and he said, "Let's go."

I maneuvered out of my position as fast as possible, which wasn't very fast at all, and slowly got out of the truck.

Cueball grabbed my arm, *in the same spot*, and pulled me into the compound.

"You know, I've been here before," I told him, having to double time to keep up. "So, there was no reason to try and hide the location from me."

Cueball looked over at me and gave me a mean grin. "I know."

Asshole.

We walked in and down a hallway, into the kitchen I'd been in once before.

"Bathroom?" I asked, trying to keep my tone even and not whiny or pleading.

He grabbed a beer out of the fridge and pointed the neck toward a door off to the left.

I hurried over there before he could change his mind or someone else came in and distracted things.

I opened the door and cringed. It was bad. *Really bad.* But I clenched my nostrils so I couldn't smell, put copious amounts of toilet paper on the seat, and did my best to hover and go quickly.

I even shut my eyes and imagined I was in a pretty pristine bathroom that was cleaned and sanitized daily.

There was no soap, so I put the water on hot and scalded my hands until they felt clean.

"Thanks," I said as I joined Cueball in the kitchen.

He was still standing by the island, drinking his beer, and he'd laid a store-bought pie on the counter. He looked pointedly at it, then back at me with a big smile.

Last time I was here he'd given me a piece of chocolate cake, but rather than eating it, I'd ended up with my face smashed into it.

"I think I'll pass," I said easily.

"Probably the smart choice," he quipped, the lifted his chin toward the hallway. "Go."

He came up behind me and pushed me on the shoulder toward another door.

"Oh, not the basement," I groaned.

We went down the steep stairs in the dark, then a door opened into a dimly lit room. This time the chair in the corner was empty, with handcuffs hanging from chains wrapped around the arms of the chair.

"You don't have to handcuff me," I began, panicked.

The sound of footsteps on stairs and a door slamming and locking had me spinning back around to see I was now alone in the dingy basement.

I looked around, hoping to find either a way to escape or a weapon.

The windows were high, small, and had bars on them. The only other door was the one with a deadbolt and two locks on it, which had once contained Cade chained to the wall inside, and I had no intention of going in there.

Other than the chair and handcuffs, there was a TV

tray and a bunch of piles of what looked like mouse droppings.

I sighed and looked to the stairs. I'd heard him lock the door so there was no use going up and trying it. And the only people who'd hear me knocking and yelling would be Diablos, so I may as well save my breath.

I crossed to the chair, wiped it off with my hand, and sat with a heavy plop.

I was really in it this time...

I wondered if Bea had been able to hear anything from my phone in the car. If she'd gotten any of the names or the confessions they'd made, because the wire was toast, along with my phone.

It was the only chance I had of being found unless someone had seen something. But even if they had ... in this area, people knew what would happen if they snitched on the Diablos, and it was nothing that could be helped with stitches.

I heard a sound and turned my head to see a small white mouse stick its head out of a hole in the corner.

"Hey, little buddy," I cooed. "What are you looking for?"

His beady eyes darted to me, and he paused.

"Probably some food, huh?"

I heard the lock click and the door open and told the mouse, "*Run!*"

Either he understood me, or he had a good sense of self-preservation, because he scurried back where he'd come from.

"You talking to yourself?" Cueball asked as he barreled down the stairs carrying something in his hand. "You only been down here like ten minutes, and you're already going crazy?"

I didn't respond, just kept my eyes warily on him.

He pulled a bottle of water and a wrapped sandwich out of a bag and put them on the tray. Then turned and started to leave again.

"Hey, how long are you gonna keep me here?" I asked.

"As long as it takes," he replied, and went back up the stairs.

"Can I at least get a t-shirt or something?" I asked, clutching my shirt closed with one hand.

He didn't answer, I just heard the snick of the lock. I got up and went to pick up the sandwich. It was from a grocery store and was sealed, so I figured it was okay.

I went back to the chair with the food and water and figured I'd better eat so I could keep my strength. Who knew how long I'd be here or when someone would give me food again?

After opening the sandwich, I pulled off some of the

bread and tossed it into the corner where the mouse had been. When his head popped back out, we sat there and enjoyed a meal together.

Chapter Twenty-Two

Since the floor was suspect, I did my best to sleep in the chair, but it was impossible. Either my head was falling back, or my back was in an awkward position.

I finally gave up and sat up in a huff.

I was hungry, tired, and cranky. Not even the little mouse scurrying across the room lifted my spirits.

I wondered how long I'd been there.

My stomach felt so empty that I was reminded of the time I tried to do a three-day detox and ended up detoxing myself right out of a stomach lining.

I did not do well without food.

I thought of my Little Debbie snack cake again and wanted to cry.

When I heard movement at the top of the stairs, I

jumped up and rushed over in time to meet Cueball before he was at the bottom of the stairs.

He threw a shirt at me, and I turned around as I eased out of my ruined shirt and slipped his over my head.

It smelled like cigarettes and beer, but at least my breasts were no longer on display.

"How long are you gonna keep me down here with no food and no place to sleep?" I asked as I turned back around. "This is inhumane, and I really should tell you that Cade is going to be supremely pissed when he finds out the conditions I was kept in."

Cueball's look was incredulous when he said, "It's been maybe three hours. Jesus, you're a piece of work. How the hell your old man puts up with you is beyond me. It's still the same damn day as when we grabbed the Jag. I don't think the sun's even went down yet."

"*Oh...*"

"I was coming down to say you could either stay down here for the night unchained, or I can put you in one of the rooms but I'm handcuffing you to the bed."

A bed sounded good, but at the mention of handcuffs I shot him a look.

He looked me up and down in distain and said, "You wish. You're a bit too geriatric for me."

Hey.

"That's not what you said at that bar in Copper Creek County."

Cueball just snorted and asked, "What's it gonna be?"

"The bed," I replied, knowing otherwise I'd never get a wink of sleep.

"C'mon."

I followed him up the stairs and down a hallway that had a bunch of doors on both sides. About midway down the hall, he opened one and gestured for me to go inside.

"What about food? Are you planning on feeding me dinner?" I asked as I walked past him into the small room that had a twin-size bed and a small dresser.

"Seriously, you're hungry again?"

"Yeah."

He muttered under his breath what sounded like, "*High-maintenance bitch,*" then said, "Stay here," and closed the door behind me.

When I heard him lock it from the other side, I wondered why I'd need to be handcuffed if it was gonna be locked anyway, and decided I'd ask him when he came back. Maybe he'd grow so annoyed with me he'd just let me go.

The bed was stripped bare and had a few stains on it, so I remained standing while I waited for Cueball to come back.

What felt like a lifetime later, the door unlocked and Cueball stepped back inside.

"Here," he said, thrusting a bowl of potato salad at me.

I looked in the bowl and asked, "That's it?"

"Take it or leave it," he said with a scowl, reaching to take it back.

I clutched the bowl to my chest and asked, "Can I get a sheet?"

He moved to the dresser, opened the top drawer, and threw the sheet he pulled out onto the bed.

"That all?" he asked.

"I should probably go to the bathroom before you lock me back in here."

Cueball rolled his eyes and asked, "Anything else, Duchess?"

"Uh ... if the door locks from the outside, why do I need to be handcuffed?"

"'Cause I half believe you'll pull some Houdini shit and disappear in the night, and I can't have you running off to your cop friends and ruining our business."

"You can't keep me here forever," I protested.

"God forbid. No, we just need time to figure out what to do with your ass."

"What does that mean? What are the options?"

Cueball's face turned scary.

"Give you a beating until you promise to keep your mouth shut, sell you to the highest bidder, or kill you."

Shit. None of that sounds good.

"I choose door number four, please. I've been trafficked before, and I didn't like it. And neither a beating nor death sound fun, so..."

"And what's behind door number four?" he asked.

"I promise to keep my mouth shut with no beating."

"I don't believe you. Now eat so you can piss, and I get be done with you for the day."

I shoveled the potato salad in my mouth with the spoon he'd put in the bowl and then handed it back to him. After he escorted me back to the worst bathroom in the history of the world, he literally handcuffed me to the post of the twin bed and left me in the dark as he locked me in.

I'm not gonna lie, I had a few panicky moments and had to calm myself down. But eventually exhaustion hit, and I drifted off to sleep.

Chapter Twenty-Three

I woke up startled and scared, my heart pounding and a sick feeling in my stomach.

Not sure what the cause was, I took a gulp of air and tried to hear above my rapid heartbeat.

Shouting.

I heard many voices shouting, some running, and – oh my God – were those gunshots?

I scooted back on the bed until my back was against the frame, my arm in an awkward position due to the cuffs.

The shooting stopped and was followed by loud pounding and banging, as if someone was kicking in doors and they were slamming against the wall. I held my breath as it got closer until I knew my door was about to be next.

I squeezed my eyes shut as the door practically splintered, and then peeked out of one eye and saw the most glorious vision I'd ever seen.

Cade was standing in the doorway, backlit and looking like an avenging angel.

Boy, he looks really mad.

"Cade," I cried, tears pricking my eyes.

He stalked into the room, put his hand behind my head, and kissed me like he hadn't seen me in years.

"Let's get out of here," he growled.

I moved my hand so that the handcuff clanked against the post.

His eyes darted to it and his scowl deepened.

"Which one?" Cade asked, and knowing what he meant, I said, "Cueball."

He left me there but was back moments later with the key in his hand. Once he'd unlocked the handcuff, he pulled me into his arms and picked me up off of the bed.

After a great hug, which made me feel a million times better, Cade put me on my feet and said, "Let's go."

He grasped my hand in his and walked me out of the room and down the hall.

When we stepped over Cueball's body, I asked, "Are they dead?" Not sure if the answer terrified me as much as it probably should.

"Nah, just knocked out," he replied as we walked around more comatose biker men and out the door.

"I heard gunshots," I told him as I hurried to keep up.

"That was them, not me. I promised Bea *no bodies*."

As we walked around the side of the building, I was reminded of the last time we'd escaped from the property and seriously hoped we never came back a third time.

Cade's bike was tucked behind some trees, and after he was seated, I happily got on behind him and held on as tight as I could.

The ride home was perfect. I felt free and safe and so grateful for the man I married.

That changed as soon as the bike pulled up to our house and we got off.

"What the fuck were you thinking?" he asked just as I was about to throw my arms around him.

I kept my arms by my side and asked, "*Excuse* me?"

"*Jesus Christ, Lila.*" He ran his hand over his head and looked at me with exasperation. "You shoot me a text that says you're working a case with Bea and that you'd be home for dinner, and then never show up."

"It's not my fault–" I began, but he wasn't done.

"And then I call Bea and she tells me the case is car

jackings where women are drugged and left at a hospital."

I figured it best to keep my mouth shut until he was finished.

"The same car-jackings that I know the fucking Diablos are pulling because I've been tracking their movements ever since we heard they were making big moves and gearing up for payback after what happened."

"Well, how was I supposed to know that?" I asked, despite my internal vow to keep quiet. "I was gonna tell you about the case, but we were both getting pulled away for work. It's what I told you I wanted to talk to you about."

"When shit's that dangerous, Lila, you find the time to tell me."

"We kept getting interrupted, by your parents, by your club..."

His glare would have frightened anyone who wasn't me.

"You know it's true," I argued.

"I also know there are plenty of times you could have, *should have*, brought it up. And you don't volunteer to put yourself into a situation that dangerous."

"We didn't know it was the Diablos, which was the whole point of the undercover mission."

"You still knew women were getting drugged."

This was true.

"I cannot believe Bea was okay with this," he said angrily.

"Don't be mad at Bea," I pleaded. "She's under a lot of stress with work and Shannon and the adoption. She thought she'd covered all the bases with the wire and all of her rules, but we didn't know it was the Diablos."

"Do you know how scared I was?" he asked, and I could see his fury was starting to fade.

"I'm sorry. So sorry, believe me. I was scared too. I almost died when I saw Cueball and Scam." At the look on his face I said, "Not literally."

"Come here," he said, and I eagerly walked into his arms. "I swear, Lila, you're gonna be the death of me."

"Does Bea know you came after me? She must have been freaked."

"Yeah, I told her after I tore her a new one."

Aww, poor Bea.

"What's gonna happen now?" I asked.

To which Cade replied, *"Fucking war!"*

Chapter Twenty-Four

"Oh my gosh, Lila, I can't believe all that happened," Carmen said, clutching my hand a little too tightly, her face full of concern.

"I honestly thought Cade was going to strangle me," Bea added, holding my other hand a bit more gently, but not much.

"I'm just lucky Cade was already aware of what the Diablos were doing and knew where to find me."

"That's another story," Bea said, and I knew she wanted to ask why Cade hadn't come to the police with any information he'd had but didn't want to stress me out any further. At least, not yet. "I could only hear muffled sounds at first and then I heard a man say my name and another voice ask if you were working with the cops, and then they hung up and I nearly lost my mind. I thought I'd gotten you killed."

I squeezed her hand and said, "But you didn't. And in a funny way I'm almost lucky it was the Diablos and not some other nasty crew. They know me and that I'm Cade's old lady, so that kept them from hurting me. It also made them abduct me, which wasn't pleasant, but everything worked out in the end. Except they took my purse, so now I have to cancel all my cards and get a new license ... and a new phone."

"At least *those* things are all replaceable. *You* aren't," Carmen said with feeling.

"Thanks, babe, and thanks for the cupcakes. You're a doll."

"I figured it was a cupcake emergency," she said with a small smile, still unsettled by everything.

"You got that right!"

"Bran wanted to come see how you were doing, too, but I told him to wait a bit and let it be just us today."

"Tell him we'll have a girls' night soon," I replied. Bran was the only man allowed at girls' night. I mean, Cade would be invited if he wanted to be, but he'd rather eat razors than hang out with us while we get drunk, gossip, and dance the night away. He did appreciate what happened *after* girls' night, which usually consisted of me tearing off his clothes.

"Oh, goody, it's been so long," Carmen said, her tone getting excited.

"What do you think, Bea, you ready for a night out?"

Bea sighed and ran her hand over her face. "I could sure use one."

"Do you think Shannon will join us?" I asked gently.

Bea caught my eye and shook her head. "We've decided to take a break. I moved into a hotel yesterday."

"What? Oh no, Bea. Is there anything I can do?" Carmen asked.

"You don't have to stay in a hotel, you could stay with us," I told her.

Her look was wry when she said, "And listen to more of the porno I got to witness last time I stayed over? I don't think I could take it."

I snickered and said, "I'd wondered if you heard."

"I'm surprised the neighbors didn't."

"We could be quiet."

"Yeah, right," she said. "Plus, I just need to be alone right now, ya know? It gives me time to think. Plus, room service."

"Oh, I love room service," Carmen agreed. "But you could always stay with me, too. Just sayin'."

"Thanks, you're both the best. Truly. And I do appreciate it. I just need some time."

"I understand," I assured her.

"Yeah, me too," Carmen added.

Bea nodded and then asked, "Are you ready to give me your statement now, Lila? I hate to ask so soon, but the sooner I have all the info, the sooner we can get a warrant and go after the Diablos."

"Yeah, of course," I said, dropping her hand and reaching for a chocolate cupcake with white chocolate frosting and ribbons of milk chocolate on top.

She put a recorder on the table and hit record, then started asking questions. By the time I was done reliving every second of what happened, twice, backwards and forwards, she said she had all she needed.

"I'm gonna go get started on this right away. Thanks again, Lila, and I am sorry."

"Hey, it's not your fault. I practically threatened to go rogue if you didn't send me undercover, okay?"

Bea nodded and gave me a quick hug, then told Carmen she'd see her later and left us.

"When are the kids due back?" Carmen asked after Bea was gone.

"This weekend. Which is why I need to get this night out planned ASAP. Maybe Friday night?" I suggested. "I'm gonna go over to Amy May's later, since I haven't seen her or Charlie since they left the hospital. I'll talk her into it."

"Sounds good to me. I'll tell Bran."

"Cool. Anything happen at work while I was gone?" I asked her.

"I posted the position for part-time receptionist and finished up some reports. There are a couple new cases that came in, but I've already got them started so you don't need to worry. Take a couple days and rest up, okay?"

"I don't know what I ever did without you, Carmen."

"Oh, you know, you winged it," she said with a laugh.

"Ain't that the truth."

Chapter Twenty-Five

"Hello," I said in my best sing-song baby voice. "Who's the cutest baby in the whole wide world? You are ... yes, you are."

Baby Charlie just blinked up at me and passed gas.

"She's so adorable, I just want to eat her up," I told Amy May, who was currently laying on the couch with her arm flung over her eyes.

"Go for it," she replied, obviously exhausted.

"Would it perk you up if I said we want to go out Friday night for ladies' night?" I teased.

She moved her arm to peek out at me.

"You better not be messing with me."

"I'd never," I swore.

"*Jason!*" she yelled, and a few seconds later he came out of the kitchen, drying a coffee mug.

"Yeah?"

"I'm going out Friday night. You've got the kiddos."

"Sounds good," he said, pushing his glasses up the bridge of his nose and hitting himself in the face with the towel. "Oops."

"You guys doing okay?" I asked with a chuckle.

"Barely," Cassidy, their twelve-year-old, said as she walked into the room holding a book. "Yesterday I saw Dad putting his phone in the refrigerator, and Mom thinks it's cool to breast feed no matter where we are ... the library, in the car, even at the grocery store."

"When Charlie's hungry, I've got to feed her," Amy May said tiredly.

"You have bottles with breast milk in them, why can't you use those?" Cassidy asked.

"Because those are for your father to use when I'm gone."

"You're never gone," Cassidy protested.

"Okay, so I forget them. Sue me."

Cassidy shook her head and said, "So embarrassing." Then asked, "When will Lena be home on Saturday?"

"Uh, I'm not sure," I said honestly. I just knew they'd be home Saturday.

Cassidy sighed and said, "I'll text her," and wandered back out of the room.

"How's that going?" I asked Amy May, as Jason

turned on his heel and kind of floated back into the kitchen.

"Despite what you just witnessed, she's actually really good with Charlie. She likes to rock with her and will come looking for her as soon as she wakes up."

"That's great."

"Yeah ... I'm thinking of going back to work sooner rather than later," she said suddenly.

"What? How soon?"

"A week, maybe two. The storefront's been really picking up and I feel terrible leaving Jordan with all the work. If I go back at least part time, I can help her out."

"What about Charlie?" I asked, looking down at the now dozing baby's sweet face.

"All she does right now is eat, sleep, and poop. She can do that at the bakery, or here with Jason. We've been talking about splitting days so we can both get some work done."

"Are you sure you're ready?"

"I will be. I mean, I'm still sore, but mostly I'm just tired because the little bug wakes up every two hours."

"I barely remember what that's like," I said, even though we'd had two little buggers taking turns sleeping and feeding. I remember it well enough to know I'd said I didn't want to do it again.

"The lack of sleep is the only reason I haven't laid

into you over what went down the last two days," she said, eyeing me again.

"Oh, you know about that?" I asked. I'd hoped she'd been one of the few who hadn't been worried.

"Cade called looking for you. Then Carmen called. And finally, Bea brought me up to date after I sent her a barrage of texts."

"I'm sorry."

"I'm just glad you're okay. You're kind of the glue that holds us all together, you know? None of us would be okay if something happened to you."

Touched, I said, "*Aww...*"

"Don't *aww* me, just promise you'll stop doing such crazy stuff."

"I'll *try*," I said, but didn't even sound convincing to myself.

"Mm-hm."

"Do you want some coffee or anything, Lila? Sorry I didn't ask before," Jason said, peeking his head around the corner.

"Sure. Have any cupcakes?" I asked.

"No, sorry," he replied.

I swiveled my head toward Amy May with a gasp.

"Don't blame me, blame the nugget."

I looked down at Charlie and said, "We're gonna have to talk about this, Charlie. You must give your mom a break so she can make Auntie Lila cupcakes. You do that, and I'll buy you all the gifts and take you all the places. Deal?"

She just kept sleeping soundly in my arms.

"She gets it," I told Amy May.

"Here you go," Jason said, putting a coffee cup on the table.

"Hey, why don't you two go take a nap? I can handle this little bundle for a while."

"Really?" Jason asked, but Amy May was already off of the couch and headed toward her bedroom.

I laughed. "Yeah, I've got her."

"Thanks, Lila," he said and followed after his wife.

"Okay, Charlie, it's just you and me. How about I tell you all about the time I caught your mom and dad roleplaying at the bar..."

Chapter Twenty-Six

"We are looking so hot, we're gonna have to beat men off with a stick. Especially you, Bran," I said happily as we prepared to enter the club.

Our nights out usually consisted more of dinner and maybe hitting a bar, but since Amy May just gave birth and was able to drink again, Bea needed cheering up, and I had been rescued from *another* abduction, we figured we'd go all out and dance like we were still in our twenties.

Bran *was* looking cute in his tight-fitting jeans and casual Tommy Bahama-style button up – *Carmen must have dressed him* – while she was in a sweet little red dress with black heels. Amy May and Bea had opted for jeans as well, but while Amy May paired hers with booties and a blouse that displayed her currently amble bosom, Bea wore a form-fitting tank and Dr. Martins.

Cynthia and I were both wearing maxi dresses, and I had a little coverup just in case it was chilly when we left.

"I'm so excited," Carmen gushed. "I haven't been dancing in forever."

We went inside and were escorted to the table I'd splurged on to have reserved for us. It was worth the cost to me to have a place to sit and keep our things when we were on the dance floor, rather than fighting with the other patrons to try and find a spot. Plus, it was around a corner so we could actually hear each other talk.

"Wow, Lila, fancy," Amy May said happily as she waived the server over.

"I try," I teased, flipping my hair over my shoulder. I'd left it down and curly but had a hair tie for when it got too hot. My purse was like Mary Poppins' bag at this point. If I needed it, it was gonna be in there.

"Can we get shots of tequila along with our drinks, please," Amy May said, causing Bea to look at me in panic. "You can put them on my tab."

Welp looks like things are getting crazy tonight.

Everyone else placed their drink orders – beer, bourbon, a cosmopolitan, a margarita, gin and tonic, and a tequila sunrise. I decided to stick with tequila since Amy

May had ordered shots and maybe I wouldn't be too hungover in the morning.

After we all downed our shots and sipped on our drinks for a few, the music called to us and Cynthia, Amy May, Bea, and I all headed to the dance floor, while Bran and Carmen promised to meet us in a few minutes.

We danced as a group and ignored any attempts by men to try and grind up on us or intrude on our party.

As I lifted my hair off my nape and put it up in a bun, I saw Carmen move through the crowd toward the DJ. He leaned down so he could hear her, and when he nodded, she gave him a grin, then turned to Bran and gave him a thumb's up.

Once the song ended, the DJ put on some reggaeton, and Carmen and Bran headed to the middle of the floor. Then they started to move. Pretty soon everyone on the dance floor had scattered to give them room and were standing around in a circle watching as Carmen and Bran danced a salsa.

"Oh my gosh, they're so good," Amy May said as we watched. "Did you know they could do that?"

I shook my head. "No, I had no idea, but now I wanna learn."

"They're amazing," Bea said.

I looked to see Cynthia's reaction, but she'd been approached by a handsome young man who looked about ten years younger than us, and they began to do the salsa as well.

We watched for a while, then I looked at my two best friends and asked, "Want to grab another drink?"

"Hell, yeah," Amy May replied, and Bea nodded vigorously.

We pushed our way through the crowd and back to our table, where our server met us and took our drink orders.

"Can we get a round of water for everyone, and do you guys serve food here too?" Bea asked.

"We've got some apps," she replied, pointing to a QR code on the table.

I scanned it and called out the options to Bea and Amy May.

"Can we get the buffalo cauliflower?" Bea asked.

"And the spinach artichoke dip," Amy May added.

"Oh, and the soft pretzels with cheese and grainy mustard," I told the server with a smile. "Thanks so much." Then I looked at my girls and said, "That should soak up some of the tequila."

Bea laughed and said, "I hope so," then took a sip of her beer.

"I'm so happy we're doing this," Amy May said with a grin. "It's nice to be out with adults and not have spit up in my hair."

"I bet," I laughed, then glanced up at Bran and Carmen as they joined us and said, "You guys are amazing. Where'd you learn to dance like that?"

"We've been taking lessons," Carmen said, her cheeks flushed.

"Don't worry, she's bringing water," Bea told her.

"And food," Amy May added.

"Awesome. You guys are the best!"

When the server came back with the drinks, everyone gulped water appreciatively.

"So, Bea, how's everything going with the adoption?" Amy May asked, taking a sip of her fresh margarita.

There was an awkward pause where you could have heard a pin drop despite the music playing around us.

Amy May caught the vibe and looked confused. "What? What's going on?"

Bea cleared her throat and explained, "Things haven't been great on the adoption front. In fact, Shannon and I are taking a break from it all … including each other."

"*Oh my God, Bea,*" Amy May cried, putting her drink down and leaning over to hug our friend. "Why didn't you say something? Do you need anything? Where are you staying? You could stay with us."

"I didn't want to bother you with it right now. You just had Charlie and you guys have your hands full."

"Hey, I'm never too busy for you, you know that, right?"

Bea gave her a grateful smile and said, "I do, yes. But I'm happy in a hotel for now."

"Are you sure?"

Bea nodded.

"Okay." A few moments later Amy May said, "I'll be right back, have to go to the restroom."

"You want company?" I asked her.

"Nah, I'm good."

After she left, Bea turned to me and said, "You should probably go after her."

"Why?"

"You know Amy May; she's probably feeling bad about talking about Charlie and stuff now that she knows the adoption's off. And maybe feeling left out of the loop..."

"You're right. I'll go check on her," I said, getting to my feet a little unsteadily. Looked like those drinks were already starting to kick in.

I went to the back of the club and was happy to see there wasn't a line for the bathroom.

"Amy May," I called as I pushed the door open and walked inside. "You good?"

I heard a grunt and then a flush, and then Amy May came out of the last stall.

"Yeah, I just had to express some milk real quick. It was starting to get painful."

"What do you mean, do you have your pump?" I asked, confused since her hands were empty.

Amy May giggled and said, "No, I just sprayed it into the toilet."

"What?" I asked with a laugh. "You did?"

She shrugged. "I had to relieve the pressure somehow."

"How do you feel now?"

"Much better."

"Well, that's good then," I said, leaning against the counter as she washed her hands. "I hope the food is there when we get back. That tequila shot is hitting hard."

"You gonna go to the bathroom while you're here?"

I looked into her pretty eyes and said, "That's probably a good idea."

Luckily, by the time we rejoined our friends, the food, and Cynthia, were waiting at the table.

"Yay, bread," I cried as I plopped in my seat and tore a chunk of the pretzel off and dipped it in cheese. "Yum!"

"We ordered a few more appetizers," Bran said as he dipped a chip.

"Awesome," Amy May chimed in.

We ate, we drank, and we danced some more, until eventually our age caught up with us and we realized it was time to go.

"Let me text Cade real quick," I said as we were divvying up the bill.

"We can take you home," Bran offered.

"That's okay. He's gonna come on his bike and we're going to take the long way home, if you know what I mean," I said, giving him a wink.

He looked perplexed. "I don't actually."

"Don't worry, honey, I'll show you later," Carmen said, and everyone started giving them a hard time.

"Oh, Bran's getting lucky tonight..."

"Carmen's gonna show it to him..."

By the time we made it outside we were all in hysterics. Except Bran, the poor dear, he still looked confused.

I heard the roar of Cade's motorcycle and looked up to watch him ride toward me.

"Damn, he's hot," I said with a sigh.

"He sure is," Amy May agreed.

"Gorgeous," Cynthia added.

Bran looked at Carmen, who made like she was locking her mouth shut and throwing away the key.

Cade parked next to us, got off the bike, and strode over to join us.

"You ladies have fun?" he asked, then looked at Bran and said, "Braswell."

"Wilkes," Bran replied.

Guys are weird.

Everyone agreed that they'd had a blast as I threw my arms around him.

"Hi," I said, looking up into his handsome face with a tipsy grin.

"Hey, darlin'."

I heard the roar of pipes again. This time very loudly, like there were a lot of bikes headed our way.

"Are we getting an escort?" I asked him.

"No," he said, furrowing his brow.

We both turned to look toward the street, and just as I noticed it was the Diablos, Cade pushed me behind him and yelled, "Get down!"

Seconds later I heard shots being fired and felt Cade's body jolt against mine.

Chapter Twenty-Seven

Everything seemed to happen all at once.

We fell to the ground and Cade rolled so that he landed on the bottom and his body softened my blow. My mind was a mess as I tried to comprehend what was going on. I pressed my hand to Cade's chest as I lifted myself up and saw him gasping up at me.

"Cade ... *what?*"

I felt something sticky and wet and pulled my hand away to see it was covered with blood.

I heard Bran on the phone with 911, telling them we needed an ambulance, and I was vaguely aware of Amy May and Carmen crying as they held each other.

"Put pressure on the wound!" Bea shouted, and I realized she was talking to me even as she was on the phone with someone else. Her precinct, I assumed, since she was giving them the Diablos' location.

I pulled my coverup out of my purse and balled it up and pressed it against the wound in Cade's chest, using my weight to hold it tightly. I learned this in one of the classes I'd taken when I'd become a PI, because I thought it would be good to know, not because I thought I'd have to put those skills to use on my husband.

"Talk to him, Lila," Cynthia said from somewhere behind me. "Keep him awake."

"Hey, baby," I managed through the tears that were streaming down my face. "The ambulance will be here any minute, okay, and they'll get you all fixed up. So, you just hang on, okay?"

I heard sirens in the distance and said, "See that, they're already here."

"Lila," he gasped.

"No," I said with a sob, leaning down to kiss his cheek before whispering in his ear, "Don't try to talk. I love you. I love you so much. You're going to be fine."

"Ma'am? Ma'am, we'll take it from here."

Someone grabbed me by the shoulders and got me out of the way so the paramedics could put Cade on the stretcher and load him into the ambulance. They took over first aid once they were inside, and I pulled away from the hands that held me and jumped into the back.

"He's my husband," I told them, and the young man told me to sit on the bench and let them take care of him.

"We'll meet you at the hospital," Bea called out as they shut the doors.

Cade had an oxygen mask covering his mouth and he looked so pale, he barely looked like himself.

My stomach clenched painfully, and I wished I hadn't had so much tequila. I lifted my hand to wipe the tears from my face, but saw they were still covered in blood and let them fall back in my lap.

Once we arrived at the hospital, I hopped out and was told they were taking him back and I'd have to wait.

It was like an out-of-body experience. I was standing in a white hallway with florescent lights watching Cade get wheeled away until the door closed, shutting me away from him.

"Ma'am, let me show you where you can wait. And when you're up to it, there's some paperwork we need you to fill out."

I let the stranger lead me down another hallway and into a room identical to the waiting room we'd been in while we'd anticipated little Charlie's arrival. It was exactly the same, but completely different.

Eventually I looked up and everyone was there. They must have been right behind us.

And then Shannon came, and Cade's parents, who

looked utterly distraught and lost, and Alani, who was making sure they were comfortable. Finally, members of his MC came in, some of them stopping to talk to me briefly.

But I honestly had no idea what anyone said to me, as the hours went on and I sat there numb.

I knew I should go comfort Cade's parents or tell Alani her brother was going to be fine, but I'd been staring at the same stain on the wall in front of me for God knew how long and it was keeping me sane.

"Delilah..."

"Honey..."

"Hm?" I asked, tearing my eyes away from the wall to look at Amy May.

"I talked to Eric last night and they were able to get the first flight out this morning. He'll be bringing the kids straight here."

"Okay."

"Honey, I think we should go get you cleaned up before they get here."

I followed her worried gaze down to my stained hands.

"Oh..."

"Come here," she said, putting her hand on my arm to help me up.

She led me to the bathroom down the hall and

turned on the water for me, then started lathering my hands and forearms with soap.

"Rinse," she said, and I did as instructed.

I looked in the mirror, and then, not wanting to look at the state I was in, I glanced at Amy May and noticed her blouse was all wet.

"What happened?" I asked.

She looked down and said, "Oh, I leaked. Jason is on his way with a change of clothes, and the pump, so I can pump and dump."

After a few moments, she asked, "Hey, did I tell you about the time I was feeding Charlie and she came unlatched mid-stream?"

I shook my head.

"Well, the milk kept coming and it ended up squirting her in the face," she said with a laugh.

I started laughing too, which turned into hysterical laughing, which ended with me sobbing uncontrollably.

"Oh no," I heard Carmen say as I felt arms hold me tight and her scent surrounded me.

"Jason's here," Bea told Amy May, and then she joined in the hug.

"Thanks, you got her?" Amy May asked.

"We've got her."

And they did.

Chapter Twenty-Eight

By the time I got back to the waiting room I felt better equipped to handle things. Yes, I was still freaked and devastated and worried, but I was no longer numb.

I moved to Cade's parents to give them each a hug and assure them everything would be all right, even though I had no idea if that was true or not, then went around the room touching base with everyone and thanking them for being there.

When I got to Cade's previous VP and now president, Sledge, he looked me dead in the eye and said, "Your man's a warrior. No way some fuckin' Diablos are going to put him down," and I found his words oddly comforting.

I nodded and made my way back to my seat, suddenly feeling utterly exhausted.

Before I was even settled, Elin and Elena came running into the room and straight into my arms.

"Mom, is he gonna be okay?" Elena asked tearfully.

I kissed the tops of each of their heads and held them tightly.

"I'm sure he will be, but we haven't heard anything from the doctors since they took him back for surgery."

I caught Eric's gaze as he and Mary came in and found available seats. I gave him a small smile and he lifted his chin in response.

I looked around the room and took in the people who were our family. It had been at least twelve hours since we'd arrived, and everyone was in various poses. Some with their heads back against the wall as they dozed, some cuddled together, while others had found a spot on the floor and simply laid out.

Bea and Shannon stood and came over to me.

"Lila, we're gonna run out and get some food for everyone. Do you want anything specific?" Bea asked.

I shook my head and managed a smile. "No, anything would be great. I appreciate it."

"Of course. Let us know if you hear anything before we get back."

"I will. Thanks, Bea."

I looked at the clock and realized we'd all missed breakfast and were well into lunchtime and decided it was time to go and try and find some answers.

"Babes, can you guys go see your grandparents for a minute, give them some love? I'm going to go find a nurse."

They nodded and moved to Cade's parents as I stood and went out to the nurse's station.

As I approached, a doctor looked up and asked, "Mrs. Wilkes?"

"Yes, that's me," I said, eagerly.

"I was just about to come find you and let you know that Mr. Wilkes is in recovery. It was touch and go for a while there, but your husband is strong and pulled through. He's going to need a lot of rest, but he's going to be fine."

"*Oh, thank God.* Thank you so much," I gushed, my eyes filling with tears. "Can I see him."

"He's being moved to a room now and once he is settled a nurse will come out and get you to take you to him."

"Thank you," I said, taking his hand and shaking it vigorously.

"It's my pleasure," he replied, then turned and walked away.

I stood there for a few minutes, shaking with relief, and then hurried toward the waiting room to relay the good news.

"He's going to be okay!" I cried as I entered.

There was a collective gasp and then cheers as everyone stood and started hugging each other. Well, except for the MC guys, they just clapped each other on the back.

I accepted everyone's hugs and well wishes as I kept one eye on the entrance, waiting for the nurse who would take me to Cade. When she finally came, I practically leapt at her, eager to see for myself that he was all right.

"Mrs. Wilkes?"

"Lila, yes," I said as I joined her.

"Please come with me," she said, then her voice got louder as she told the room. "He'll only be allowed two visitors at once. Lila will be out to let you know when you can start rotating in. Visiting hours end at six and begin again at eight in the morning. Please try and limit your time, as Mr. Wilkes needs to get as much rest as possible."

I tried to be patient while she gave the necessary information, but it took all my willpower not to yank her out of the room and insist she take me to Cade immediately.

After answering a few questions, we were on our way. My heart was in my throat when we finally reached the door that had "Wilkes" on the label. And when I opened the door, my eyes scanned the dimly lit room until they fell on the bed near the window.

His eyes were closed and there were machines beeping, but his coloring looked much better, and I could see his chest rise and fall.

I nearly fainted with relief.

I moved slowly toward him, careful to be quiet so I wouldn't wake him. Once I was at his bedside, I looked over his large body as if double checking everything was as it should be, and it was, except for the bandage I could see on his chest, peeking out of the opening in his hospital gown.

The thought struck me that he was going to *hate* the fact they had him in that gown. He usually slept naked, but I was sure I could find him some basketball shorts or something at home that I could bring in.

My eyes filled again as I took in his face, which looked peaceful in sleep, and I wondered how many gallons of tears I'd shed since last night.

I was surprised I wasn't dehydrated.

"*Lila,*" Cade whispered, and my gaze flew to his.

I leaned down and kissed him gently, then gave him

a sort-of hug while making sure I didn't do anything that may hurt him.

I pulled back and looked into his eyes as I pushed the hair back off of his forehead.

"*Hey, baby*. You're going to be just fine."

Chapter Twenty-Nine

"Save me ... Cade is the worst patient in the history of patients!"

"Come on, Lila, he can't be that bad. But he *was* just shot after all," Carmen said quietly, probably afraid he'd overhear.

"I know, and I'm so happy he's okay," I told her. "But if he whines about being bored, or complains about my food one more time, I'm gonna lose it."

"Have you called his mom?" she asked.

"No. I mean, they've stopped by a couple times..."

"When I'm sick or hurt, I always want my mom. And moms are the only ones who love taking care of their kids. They *live* for that stuff. I bet if you asked her for help, she'd be over here lickety split, and happy as a clam about it. Then you could come to the office for a few hours to get a break and Cade can be pampered by the *one* person who won't get annoyed by the fact that men are big babies when they're incapacitated."

"Carmen, you're a genius! I mean it, this could really save my marriage," I told her, giving her a big kiss on the mouth before running to find my phone.

"Lila?" Cade asked when he saw me pass by the room. "Can you bring me a beer and an ice pack? Oh, and maybe some food, I'm hungry."

"No to the beer, but yes to the rest," I called back cheerfully as I took my phone off the charger.

I caught his grumble over the no-beer decree but I gleefully ignored it as I dialed his mother.

"Lila, is everything okay?" she asked when she answered. This was her new version of "hello." Ever since the shooting she was terrified every call was bad news.

"Yes, everything is great. I was just calling because it's been over a week now and I really need to go into the office–"

Before I could even finish the sentence, she said, "I'm on my way."

I hadn't replied before she hung up.

"That worked like a charm," I told Carmen when I joined her in the kitchen. "I'll take Cade his lunch and an ice pack and as soon as she gets here, we can go into the office."

"Awesome, it's been lonely there without you," Carmen said. "Which is why I dropped in on you like this ... I hope that's okay."

"You're always welcome, you know that."

"I know, it's just, you have so much going on I was trying to give you space."

"Please, don't. I'm not the kind of person who craves solitude. I need people, and noise, and not to be a nursemaid. I'm not the kind of person who likes to coddle or is even very good taking care of others in that way. Not even with the kids. Eric was always the one they went to when they were sick. Not to say I don't care; I'm just maybe missing that gene ... the caregiver."

"Hey, you have been the caregiver, but it's okay to need help. We all have our strengths, and yours is being a badass."

"Aww, that's sweet."

I finished making Cade's sandwich, grabbed a bag of Doritos, and took that along with a bottle of water and an ice pack to the bedroom, where he was laid up watching TV.

"Here, honey," I said as I put the items on the tray table I'd bought for him to have next to the bed, so he'd have easy access to things. "Your mom's going to come over and stay with you while I go into the office."

"Okay, cool. Maybe I can get her to make that soup she used to make for me when I was sick," he said, his dark eyes meeting mine.

"Oh, and ask for some Loco Moco, too," I said eagerly.

His lips curved up. "Okay, darlin', and, hey, sorry for being such a pain in the ass."

I leaned over and gave him a kiss. "It's okay. It's much better than the alternative."

"You got that right."

"Call me if you need anything, all right?"

"I'll be fine, don't worry. Ma will have everything covered … You may have a hard time getting rid of her."

"She's welcome to stay as long as she wants," I assured him.

"Great," Ma said from the doorway, startling me. "I brought some things just in case."

She came in and started fussing with his pillows and I took that as my cue to leave.

"Love you," I said before walking out.

"Love you, too," they both replied.

Carmen was waiting for me in the living room, and I noted Ma's very large suitcase on our way out the door.

Some things?

"I'll meet you at the office," I told Carmen as I headed toward my Caravan.

I parked in my parking space, feeling light for the first time since that fateful night, and gleefully let myself inside.

It looked the same but there was something about the feel and smell of the place that was exactly what I needed. Normalcy. Sure, it was still a relatively new normal, but it was all mine and I needed it.

"Hey, look who I found parking outside," Carmen said a few moments later, and I turned to see her and Bea coming inside.

"Hey, Bea, how's it going?" I asked.

"Great!" she exclaimed. "I was going to call but then I saw you driving down Main Street and figured you were headed this way."

"What's up?"

"We caught 'em, Lila," she said excitedly. "Cueball, Scam, Trot, the whole lousy lot of them."

"You did?" I said, finding the nearest chair and plopping down. It felt like a huge weight had been lifted off of my shoulders and I needed a moment to catch my breath.

"We did. The Diablos are in custody and will face charges on carjacking, abduction, and attempted murder."

"That is so wonderful!" Carmen exclaimed.

I couldn't speak. I simply dropped my head in my hands and tried to process the fact that Cueball, the monster who'd taken me and shot Cade, was off the streets for good.

When I was able to contain myself, I looked back up at Bea and said, "Thank you."

"You got it, babe."

Chapter Thirty

"I'm draggin', so I'm going to walk over to Cynthia's and get a coffee. Do you want anything?"

Carmen looked up from her computer screen.

"Hey, since when do you wear glasses?" I asked her.

She scrunched up her nose and said, "They help me see the screen better. It's tough getting older."

"They look cute," I assured her.

"Thank. And, uh, I don't know. If you see something you think I'll like, surprise me."

"You got it."

I walked outside and headed toward Main Street. The weather was perfect – high seventies with a light breeze, which made the walk very pleasant.

When I got to the bookstore, I took a moment to

appreciate Cynthia's window display, which she updated weekly. This week she was showcasing the fantasy genre. There were books, of course, but she'd also decorated with dragons, fairies, and angels to create a magical, otherworldly feeling.

It made me want to go home and watch *The Lord of the Rings*. Maybe I'd put it on and force Cade to watch with me.

I opened the door, enjoying the chimes that signaled a new arrival, and started toward the café area.

"Sweet Lila, how are you doing?" Cynthia asked, breezing toward me, her brow furrowed.

"Good," I managed as I was engulfed in a lavender-scented hug.

"And how's that rugged husband of yours?"

"He's getting stronger. He stopped using the pain pills because he didn't like the way they made him feel, so if he gets too uncomfortable, he can be a bit like a bear, but I'm happy to say the doctors think he'll be up and moving around in no time."

"Here," she said, holding out her hand so I would do the same. "Take this clear quartz crystal and put it under Cade's pillow or next to the bed. It has healing properties."

I accepted the crystal and said, "Oh, thanks so much," then put it in my pocket.

"Are you here for coffee?" Cynthia asked as she fell in step beside me.

"Yes, and maybe that delicious-looking red velvet cupcake on display there," I said, pointing at the confection. "And a chai for Carmen."

She relayed the order to her barista and asked, "How's the new office space working out?"

"Wonderful. It's really the best idea I've had in a long time. You'll have to come check it out."

"I'd love to. Carmen settling in okay?"

"Yes, she's my other great idea," I said with a laugh. "In fact, we're looking at hiring a receptionist. Part time at first, to see how it works out for all of us. Carmen posted it, but I haven't checked back to see if we've gotten any bites yet."

"You know, my sister's actually looking for part-time work and I think she'd be perfect."

"Really? Send her by and I'll give her an application and chat her up."

Wait, do we even have applications? I wondered. I needed to look into that.

"Wonderful, I'll give her a call in a bit. Her name's Dylan."

"I'll keep an eye out for her."

"Large Americano, chai, and cupcake," the barista called out.

"That's me, thanks," I said, moving for my wallet.

"It's on me this time," Cynthia said, waving my money away.

"You can't keep doing this, Cynthia, you're running a business," I protested.

"I insist." Her expression brokered no argument.

"Okay. Thank you very much. Carmen and I appreciate it."

She nodded serenely and I told her I'd see her later and let myself out.

When I walked back into the office, I called out, "I'm back," and Carmen met me in the hallway.

"I got you a chai."

"Oh, goody. Thank you," she said, taking it from me.

"Cynthia wouldn't let me pay again."

"She's so sweet."

"Do we have job applications?" I asked her.

Carmen shook her head and said, "No, not anything formal. I was just asking for their CV."

"CV ... what's that?"

"It stands for Curriculum Vitae, which is Latin for 'course of life.' It's like a resume, but longer."

"Huh, *fancy*. You learn something new every day," I said with a shrug. "But, yeah, that works."

"Why, did someone ask for an application?"

"No, but Cynthia did say she has a sister, Dylan,

which I did not know, and that she is looking for part-time work. Cynthia thinks she'd be a good fit, so I told her to have Dylan stop by."

"That'll be cool. If she's anything like Cynthia, I'm sure she'll be great."

"I hope so. It would be nice to get the position filled. In the meantime, I'm going to return some emails to prospective clients and then pick up some takeout and go home. I know I said Cade was getting on my nerves, but now I find myself missing him."

"Okay, I'll still be here for a while, so I'll lock up."

"Thanks, Carmen. I appreciate you."

"Aww, I appreciate you, too, Lila."

Chapter Thirty-One

"If I don't get out of this house soon, I'm gonna lose it."

I looked around Cade's mom, who was sitting *between us* on the couch, so I could see Cade.

"Where do you want to go?" I asked him.

"A ride, the clubhouse, the cabin ... anywhere else," he said with a scowl.

"I don't think you should be riding your motorcycle just yet," I said, even though I knew it wasn't what he wanted to hear.

"I'm fine," Cade protested, which we all knew was a lie. He *was* doing much better, but he was still sore, and although he was up and around more, he was still moving slower than usual. "Even the doc said I was healing fast, no infection or anything. It's time to stop babying me and let things get back to normal."

"Babying you? Who's babying you?" I asked ... 'cause it sure wasn't me.

Heck, I'd love for him to be recovered a hundred percent too, but he wasn't.

Cade's gaze flicked to his mother before dropping.

It had been well over a week since Ma had *stopped by to help*, and although I was grateful for her nursing Cade, and was not mad about the homemade meals and sparkly clean house, it was hard to have *alone time* with Cade.

Ma's eyes were still on the TV watching whatever car restoration show Cade had put on, but I was sure she was aware of our conversation. The woman heard everything.

Before I could broach the subject of her going back to the cabin, there was a hard knock on the front door and then it opened, and Pops came walking in.

"How's it going?" he asked, his eyes touching on his wife before landing on his son. "You feeling okay?"

"Going stir-crazy," Cade replied.

"I hear that," he said, then walked over and stopped in front of the couch. "I'm here for my wife."

That made Ma look up.

"Come back to the cabin," he pleaded. "We're

supposed to close on the house in a couple days, and Alani is either at school or locked away in her bedroom. I'm going nuts over there by myself."

"I was thinking maybe we should wait on the house," she told him.

"What? Ma, what's going on?" Cade asked.

"You need me here," she replied. "Buying a house now means moving in and furnishing it and everything. It's a lot of work and I won't be able to help you out if we close on the house now."

"Are you serious?" Pops asked with a frown.

"No, Ma, listen ... I appreciate you coming and helping out here, but I'm on the mend now and you and Pops gotta live your own lives. Don't put it on hold for me. You came out here to find a house so you could live here part time, and you found one you love, so finish what you started and get it. I'll be fine. Me and Lila can take it from here."

"Yes, we can. But we are both grateful for your help," I added.

"Okay, if you're sure," she said, and Pops took that as a *yes* and said, "I'll go get your things."

He wasn't playing around.

"There's more soup in the fridge. And I stocked up on that tea you like, Lila. It's in the pantry."

"Thank you," I said as she got up to follow after Pops

and probably make sure he didn't miss anything. Then I glanced at Cade and asked, "You sure you're okay with her leaving?"

I imagined us spending the evening with each other, eating takeout and maybe drinking some wine – Ma had had Cade on a strict no-alcohol diet – and then ending the night in bed with me gently making love to him ... *something else that hadn't happened since his injury*.

"Yeah, *Jesus*. I'm not an invalid. I don't need a fucking nursemaid and I don't need you taking over the hovering once Ma leaves. What I need is to be left alone," he said in a burst of irritation, and all of those lovely ideas I'd just had fizzled in my mind.

"You want to be alone?" I asked, standing up and glaring at him. "Fine. Sit here and stew in your misery. Butthole."

I stalked out of the room and into the kitchen where I poured *myself* a glass of wine – *up yours, Cade* – and then took it out onto the back patio.

We still hadn't figured out what to do with the space, so I took out my phone and brought up Pinterest. As I was looking at ideas and pinning them to my new *Fabulous Patio* board, Ma and Pops came in.

"We're getting ready to leave," Ma said, so I stood up and moved to give them each a hug.

"Thanks again. And let me know if you need any

help once you start getting in stuff for the house. You'll have to have a housewarming party."

"That's a wonderful idea, and you're welcome. Anytime. I know my son can be a terrible patient; if we're being honest, all men are."

Pops shrugged and said, "It's true."

"Just have patience with him. This too shall pass."

"I will," I promised, but I had my fingers crossed behind my back.

They shuffled out and I sat back down to resume my gathering décor ideas until I felt much calmer and in a better headspace. Then I decided to go ask Cade what he'd like to eat and suggest I take us on a drive or something. Maybe go have a picnic in the park.

"Babe," I called as I walked down the hall. "I've got an idea that may help your cabin fever."

He was no longer in the living room and the TV was off, so I went back down the hall to our bedroom. And when he wasn't there, I checked the kitchen.

"Cade!"

When he didn't answer, I opened the front door and stepped outside and walked down the sidewalk.

The garage was open, and his bike was gone.

"*Son of a bitch!*"

Chapter Thirty-Two

"Thanks for coming over, you guys. Not only am I happy to see you, but you being here will ensure I don't commit murder when Cade finally shows back up, so..."

I raised my glass to Amy May, Carmen, and Bea before taking a sip of the frozen beverage. I'd made a pitcher of Frosé, which we were enjoying outside as we watched the sun go down.

"Have you been able to get ahold of him?" Amy May asked from the seat beside me.

I shook my head.

"I didn't even try. He's obviously going through something right now and since he felt the need to slink off like a child, I figure he'll come back when he's ready.

In the meantime, I'm enjoying a tasty beverage with my besties and I'm not worrying about it."

"What if he like opens up his wound again, or something? Is it safe for him to be on a motorcycle already?" Carmen asked.

I waved my hand in the air. *"Not worrying about it."*

"He's smart enough not to overdo it," Bea said reassuringly. "He's probably just going crazy being all laid up and needed to feel like he was getting some control back over his life. I get it. I hate being bedridden."

"Yeah, Bea's right. He'll be fine. You can't keep a man like that down for long," Amy May agreed.

"Enough about my free bird husband, what's going on with you guys? I feel like I've been so consumed with Cade since the shooting that I haven't really checked in with you all as much as I should."

"Well, you know my house is madness right now," Amy May said with a laugh. She leaned back and stretched her legs out in front of her with a sigh. "Charlie runs that place and is running Jason and I ragged. Luckily, he's got Cassidy and Lena there tonight ... thanks for letting her stay over, by the way ... and they are both so good with Charlie."

"Yeah, of course. Elin's at his friend Mikey's house, too. I think they both needed a break from the house too. Apparently, we're all mad here."

Carmen sat up and cleared her throat, a small smile playing on her lips. "I, uh, actually have some news."

"What is it?" I asked.

"Yeah, tell us something good," Amy May encouraged.

"Bran and I are moving in together!" she exclaimed, doing a little shimmy in her seat.

"That's wonderful," Amy May gushed.

"Congrats," Bea said, lifting her glass in salute.

"Wow, that's big, Carmen. Are you planning to move into his place?" I asked.

"No, actually, we want to start fresh together, so we are looking at moving into a new place. It's a little scary, and a big commitment, but I love him and the idea of making a home together just lights me up inside."

"I love that for you. For both of you," I told her with a smile, then raised my glass and said, "To Carmen and Bran, may this next step in their lives bring them joy and be the beginning of a beautiful journey."

"Here, here."

"To Carmen and Bran."

"Thanks, guys. I love you guys so much and I can't tell you how much better my life has been since I met you all and you let me into your lives. I'm so grateful I approached Lila to do that story on her. I don't know what I'd do without you."

"It's not something you'll ever need to worry about," I assured her.

"In keeping with the good news," Bea began, and we all looked at her expectantly. "Shannon and I are working things out." There was a chorus of happy noises and she continued, "After everything happened with Cade, we realized how trivial our arguments have been and that our love for each other is the most important thing. I've moved back in and we're starting therapy on Monday."

"Oh my gosh, Bea, that's great," I said, tears coming to my eyes. "I know you two will be stronger than ever."

"So happy to hear it," Amy May agreed with a grin.

"Yay! It's going to great; I promise. Therapy is so great and once you guys really get in there and dig deep, you're going to feel better individually and as a couple."

We all looked at Carmen.

She blinked back and said, "What? I love therapy. It has really helped me manage my OCD, deal with my feelings of abandonment, and has made me able to be ready to take this big step with Branson. I'm a huge proponent of it and think everyone should do it."

We all paused when we heard the rumble of pipes, and I think each of us had visions of that night outside the club, because there was a moment of fear before we heard the bike come to a stop and turn off.

"It's okay, it's just Cade," I assured them as I got up, but I noticed everyone followed me inside and to the front door.

When Cade walked in, he paused and took in the group.

"Ladies," he said, but I noticed he had a hitch in his stride and his voice sounded a little thin.

Guessing we needed to be alone, they all said their goodbyes and headed out.

Once we were alone, Cade turned to me and said, "I think I over did it, darlin'."

I nodded and moved to support him. "Come on, let's go get you settled."

He leaned on me just enough to take some of the pressure off but not enough to crush me under his weight.

I helped him take off his leather jacket, tank, and jeans and before he laid back in bed.

"I'll go get you some water and something to eat."

"Thanks, Lila," he said, then before I could walk out called, "Lila."

"Yeah?"

"Sorry for being such a dick."

I gave him a smile and said, "Thanks. You want one of your pills?"

"Just some ibuprofen, okay?"

"Sure thing."

"Love you."

"I love you, too," I said, then continued to the kitchen to take care of my man, feeling a sense of relief that my world was right again.

Chapter Thirty-Three

"Lila, Dylan is here," Carmen said, and I glanced up to see her peeking around the corner into my office.

"Great, can you send her back?"

"Sure thing."

A few moments later, a beautiful, petite black woman came walking in. She was dressed conservatively in tailored slacks and a pretty blouse, and her dark curls were pulled back from her face.

"Hi," I said, standing and moving around my desk to shake her hand. "I'm Delilah Horton. You can call me Lila."

"Dylan. It's nice to meet you."

"Please, have a seat," I said, gesturing to one of the chairs in front of my desk. "So, you're Cynthia's sister?"

"Yeah, although since she's fourteen years older we didn't really grow up together. She's more like a second mom."

"And she said you're looking for part time work, at least initially?"

Dylan pulled a folder out of her bag and handed it to me as she replied, "Yes. I'm currently going to college full time. I'm studying Criminology and hope to join the FBI. When she told me about this job, I thought it would be a perfect fit."

"Do you have classes every day?"

"No, I take all of my courses on Tuesdays and Thursdays, so I'd be available every other day of the week."

I opened the folder and took out her resume ... or CV.

"Okay, it says you used to work as a receptionist for the Art Department at school?"

"Yes, it was part of my work study freshman year. I basically answered the phones, took messages, and did any filing, copying, and collating they needed done."

"This position would include all of that, but also requires a level of discretion. You'll be dealing with clients' personal lives and it's important that what happens at work remains here."

"I can do that," she said easily.

"Perfect. How about I give you the tour."

I escorted her out of my office and to the back first, showing her where the bathroom, back exit, and break room were, before taking her out front.

"This is where you'll be," I said, showing her behind the counter, where the high-back stool I'd ordered was waiting, along with a computer, phone with multiple lines, and filing cabinets.

Dylan nodded and looked around the space.

"So, what do you think, do you want to try it out?" I asked.

"I'd love to."

"Yay," Carmen said, immediately coming out of her office to join us as if she'd been waiting just inside for Dylan's answer. "It's so great to have you join the team."

"You already met Carmen," I said with a laugh. "It'll pretty much just be the three of us, but occasionally you'll see my husband, Cade, and Carmen's boyfriend, Bran, here helping out. Along with our friends, Amy May and Bea. We can be a crazy bunch, but you'll get used to us."

Dylan nodded politely and asked, "When would you like me to start?"

It was Monday, so I said, "How about you be here Wednesday at nine."

"I'll be here," she replied.

"Great, we'll see you then," I said as I walked her to the door.

Once she was gone, I turned to Carmen and asked, "What do you think?"

"Well, I overheard your conversation, you know, since our offices are so close together..." *Mm-hm.* "And I love the fact that she's studying to become an agent. I think she can learn a lot here that will help her with her career, and I'm sure she'll be an asset. She looked very put together, so hopefully that'll translate into her being organized and on task."

"Yeah, I think she'll do very well. I gotta say, I was expecting her to be more like Cynthia ... more boho, less preppy ... and she's so young. Is that what college students look like nowadays?"

"Well, yeah, look at Alani. She looks like she could still be in high school and she's in college."

"True," I said with a sigh. "I guess I'm just getting old."

"Hey, you're not old. You're only a few years older than me."

I frowned at her. "But you look like you're ten years younger ... your skin is flawless."

"I have a great nighttime regiment. I can give you a list of the things I use."

I shook my head and said, "There's no point. I'd

never use it. I can't tell you how many times I buy products with the intention of starting a routine, and they just end up sitting on my shelves collecting dust. Soap, water, and lotion is about all I can maintain."

"Well, I think you look great, so whatever you do is working."

"You're sweet for saying so. *A liar*, but sweet."

"What do you say we go to Jake's for lunch?" I asked her.

"I say, count me in."

We grabbed our things and locked up, then headed down the street toward the restaurant.

"Maybe we need to get one of those signs with the clock to hang on the door to say when we'll be back at the office," I mused.

"Yeah, that would be good. I can stop at the store later and grab one. Hey, how did it end up going with Cade? Did he hurt himself? He looked paler than usual when he walked in."

"He was okay but did admit to overdoing it. Still, I think it did him good to get away for a bit. He may have been feeling smothered with always having me or Ma underfoot. He'll probably do better now that he has some space, and one of the kids is usually around in case he does need something."

"Well, I'm glad you guys are doing okay. I don't like it when you fight."

I chuckled and threw my arm around her shoulder.

"Don't worry, it'd take more than a gunshot wound and bad tempers to mess up what we have."

Chapter Thirty-Four

As soon as I walked in the door, I dropped my things on the chair and pulled my hair out of the bun. Shaking it out, I ran my fingers through it, massaging my scalp to ease the ache. Then I reached under the back of my shirt to undo my bra and pulled the straps off through the sleeves and eased it out, letting it land on top of my bag.

"That's better," I muttered as I stepped out of the heels I'd worn that day, and seriously contemplated losing the pants as well.

I'd dressed up fancier than usual, due to my interview with Dylan, and missed my more casual uniform of jeans and a T-shirt.

I moved through the house, tired and hungry, to the kitchen, where I planned on pouring a glass of wine and gnawing on a block of cheese while I figured out what to do for dinner.

But before I reached the kitchen, I passed the dining room and stopped in my tracks.

The table was set with the good China, and there were flowers and candle sticks in the center.

"What in the world?" I wondered out loud as Cade entered from the kitchen and paused when he saw me.

"Hey, babe, I didn't hear you come in," he said with a grin.

I could hear music coming from the kitchen, which is probably why he didn't hear me.

He'd showered and shaved and had his long hair pulled back into a bun, and he was wearing nice jeans and a Henley that was just tight enough to have my bare breasts tightening.

Guess I should've left my bra on...

"What's all this?" I asked, unable to keep myself from smiling.

"I wanted to do something special for you to apologize for all the missed meals and broken dates, and for being such an ass over the last couple weeks. So, I made you dinner."

"Wow, it looks wonderful," I gushed as he put down the platter of barbecued chicken he'd been holding.

"There's baked beans and corn too, I'll just go grab

them. I already poured your wine," he said, then went back out of the room.

I sat down, noting the rolls and butter, but reaching for the wine instead.

"Where are the kids?" I asked as he came back in and placed the rest of the food on the table.

"They already ate," Cade said as he sat. "They said they wanted to give us some privacy so we could have a real date and went to their rooms."

"Oh, that was sweet of them," I said, then met his eyes and added, "And this is all really lovely. Thank you."

"Anytime, darlin', I should do it more. And I plan to."

"Oh?" I asked, taking a roll out of the basket he offered to me.

"Yeah," he said, looking earnest. "I had a talk with Slade and I'm stepping down from club business."

I blinked and paused because I *had not* been expecting that.

"What do you mean?"

"I'll still be part of the club and I'll ride – that'll never stop – but I'm not going to get shit done for them anymore."

"You're not going to be The Enforcer?"

"The what?"

"*The Enforcer*. That's what the Diablos call you."

"Idiots," he scoffed. "That's why they're in jail. But no, I won't be doing that work anymore. I'm strictly going to do the restoration and build work. I'll do some for them when they need it, but I was thinking I'd like to start up my own restoration business outside of the club. There's room at the cabin, plenty of land to work on, so I can start something there. What do you think?"

"I think it's great, but I have to admit I'm surprised. I thought you loved what you do."

"I love you and the kids more."

"*Cade*," I whispered, reaching my hand toward him.

He grasped it and said, "We've been through some crazy shit that last couple years, Lila, and although not all of it has been tied to my business with the club, a lot of it has. I know you love what you do and I'm not gonna ask you to stop. But maybe if we take that aspect out of the equation, shit won't be so dangerous all the time. I'd like for us to get through a year without any abductions, real or otherwise."

"That would be good," I agreed with a laugh. "I just want you to be sure this is what *you* want."

"It is. You know I love working on bikes, especially restoration. This will give me the ability to focus on that and really grow something I can be proud of."

"It'll be amazing," I assured him, clutching his hand

and leaning over so I could kiss him.

He met me halfway, eagerly accepting my offer.

I pulled back slightly and placed my hand on his cheek as I looked into his eyes.

"I love you and just want you to be happy. If this is what you want, you have my full support, you know that."

"Thanks, babe."

"Now, let's eat this amazing meal you made before it gets cold."

"Looks like you're already a little cold," Cade said with a chuckle, and I followed his gaze to see my nipples were stiff and showing beneath my sheer blouse.

"Sorry, if I'd known all the trouble you'd gone to, I would have waited until after dinner to go braless."

"I love it," he said with a grin. "Adds a certain level of sexiness to some barbecue. I think you should always go braless."

"Yeah? How about if I do this?" I asked, unbuttoning the top two buttons so he could see the swell of my cleavage.

His eyes darkened and his voice was rough when he said, "I'd say I'm no longer in the mood for chicken ... I'd like to lay you out on the table instead and feast."

I dropped my roll on my plate and said, "Go ahead. I dare you."

Chapter Thirty-Five

Cade stood up and pushed back his chair, while I did the same, and we met in a fervor of kisses and gropes. Aware of his wound, I perched myself on the edge of the table, causing silverware to fall to the ground, and wrapped my legs around his waist.

We were so hot and heavy that I didn't realize we weren't alone until I heard Elena cry out, "Oh, gross!"

Cade jumped back quickly and immediately brought his hand up to his chest as he winced at the sudden movement.

Oh my God. I'd forgotten the kids were here.

I made sure I was presentable before I turned to look at my daughter and ask, "What's up, sweetie?"

"Ugh, don't call me *sweetie* when you're being

pervy," she said with a look of disgust. "I was coming to see if you guys wanted to watch a movie tonight, but I've changed my mind."

Lena turned and went back the way she came, muttering under her breath as she walked away.

I looked back at Cade, who looked like he was trying really hard not to laugh, which made me start laughing, and then he joined in.

"Whoops," I said lightly as he helped me off the table.

We both sat back down in our seats and regained our composure.

"I'm really hungry," I murmured, picking my roll back up and tearing a piece off before popping it in my mouth.

"Famished," Cade agreed with a grin.

I reached down to pick up the silverware and put it back on the table then reached for the platter of chicken.

"Want some?" I asked, picking up a chicken breast with the tongs and offering it to him.

"Please."

I served him and then myself, before doing the same with the other dishes until we both had a little of everything. Then we dug in.

When we finished, I cleaned up while Cade went to get some rest, then I went in search of my daughter in order to apologize for the scene she'd walked in on. Cade and I were always very demonstrative, but never to the point where the kids were uncomfortable, so I felt bad about getting carried away.

Her door was shut, so I knocked before opening it a crack and peering inside.

She was sitting on her daybed listening to music and reading.

"I don't know how you can do that," I said softly as I stepped inside. "I'd be too distracted by the music to comprehend what I was reading."

Lena glanced up at me then looked back down at her book.

"Hey," I said, nudging her arm with my own as I sat beside her. "I'm sorry about before. We got kind of carried away ... We didn't mean for you to see that."

She let out a heavy sigh and put a receipt she was using as a bookmark into her book before closing it.

"Yeah, it was not cool."

"Can you forgive us?"

"Yeah, Mom, I can ... And you know I'm happy you're so happy, but please try and keep your *love* behind closed doors. I can't even imagine what Elin would have done if he was the one who walked in ... probably barfed."

I let out a giggle and then covered my mouth when she glared at me.

"Sorry," I said, swallowing my mirth. "If the offer to watch a movie is still on the table, we'd love to take you up on it. I'll make popcorn!"

"Okay, but you and Cade are sitting apart. I don't want you getting handsy again."

I laughed again. I couldn't help it, Lena was funny, and I was happy she was comfortable enough to talk with me about this kind of stuff. Amy May said Cassidy had stopped talking to her about anything at all and she was really missing having a closer relationship with her.

"Cross my heart," I promised. "Want me to grab Elin?"

She shook her head and said, "I'll tell him. You know if there's popcorn he'll be there."

"I'll make two."

I went to the kitchen and made enough popcorn to fill up two bowls, grabbed a few boxes of candy out of the cupboard, and went to join my family in the living room.

Cade was sandwiched by Lena and Elin on either side of him and Elin was telling him about some of the wildlife they'd seen on the island while on their trip. Cade was giving Elin his full attention while Lena looked for a movie to watch on the TV.

"Here's some popcorn and candy," I said, putting it all down on the coffee table. "Does anyone want me to grab them a drink before we get started?"

"Beer."

"Coke."

"Water."

I went to get us all drinks and then came back and distributed them before taking the seat next to Elena.

"*Jumanji?*" she asked.

"New or old?" Elin asked.

"Doesn't matter," she said.

"How about we do a marathon of all of 'em?" Cade suggested.

"Okay," Lena said with a smile. She loved binging stuff. Shows, movies, it didn't matter.

"*Knock, knock,*" Cade's dad called out, literally knocking on the door as he opened it.

"In here, Pops," Cade called out and seconds later, Ma, Pops, and Alani walked into the living room.

"Aloha," Pops said with a big grin.

"*Aloha,*" Elin and Lena replied, jumping up off the couch to give hugs.

We all said our hellos and Alani said, "I told them to call or text before just coming over, but I think they like the element of surprise."

"Be careful what you wish for in this house," Elena

mumbled under her breath, and I shot her a look that should have made her cringe, but she simply shrugged.

Punk.

"Once the craziness of moving in starts we'll be busy for a while, so we figured we would stop in and check on you guys now," Ma said, pulling Cade's Henley down to try and see his wound.

"You're stretching it out," he grumbled, trying to pull it back, but she swatted his hand away.

"We're about to have a *Jumanji* marathon. Do you guys want to join?" Lena asked.

"What's *Jumanji*?" Pops asked.

"Oh, you're gonna love it," she promised.

"Sounds fun," Ma said, moving to one of the recliners and claiming her seat.

"I'll make more popcorn," I said, getting up.

"I'll help," Alani offered.

"Thanks."

Once everyone had their junk food, drinks, and throw blankets, we all settled in to watch at least six hours of fun, action, and adventure. More, when after the first movie Elin insisted that *Zathura* is also part of the franchise and should be included in the binge.

Chapter Thirty-Six

"Your breakroom is kick-ass," Bea said as she walked back into the front of my office to join us. "It's stocked better than my pantry."

"Cade's been coming in and restocking. I think it gives him some kind of satisfaction to see the fridge and cupboards full. And I'm not mad about it."

"Me neither," Carmen agreed. "Although I need to do better at sticking to the healthy snacks. Those Little Debbie's just keep calling my name."

We were all together for an impromptu lunch.

Bea and Cynthia had both asked about stopping by to see the place, so I'd called Amy May and told her to come join us. Little Charlie was currently snoozing in her car seat, while the rest of us were enjoying burgers and fries from this new little joint that had recently opened on Main Street.

"How are your classes going?" Cynthia asked Dylan, who'd been working with us for a couple weeks now.

"Good," Dylan replied with a shrug, then said, "Don't touch that," when her sister started picking up stuff on her desk.

"Sorry," Cynthia said easily, then looked at us and said, "Dylan has always been very particular about her *things*."

"And Cynthia is *never* particular about *anything*," Dylan replied. "She's the messiest person I've ever met."

"I think the bookstore is charming," Amy May said, smiling at Cynthia.

"Oh, not the store. She's different when it comes to business, but in her personal life? Let's just say she's allergic to order. And forget about putting laundry away," Dylan said with a laugh.

"Hey, I know where everything is at all times," Cynthia retorted. "It may seem like chaos to you, but that's because you go crazy if your sock drawer is messy. You're so anal about your apartment that it makes me twitchy to even come over. I'm afraid I'll accidentally put a water mark on your table or something."

They stuck their tongues out at each other and I thought, *Okay, they are definitely sisters!*

"How are you enjoying working with these two, Dylan?" Amy May asked, gesturing to me and Carmen.

"She loves us," Carmen joked.

Dylan's lips turned up and she said, "It's been fun so far. I find the number of cheaters coming across the desk kind of appalling, but I'm learning a lot. Lila let me go with her on a stakeout, and Carmen makes paperwork easy. She makes my efficient heart beat."

"Aww, you're so sweet," Carmen said, placing her hand over her own heart.

"Excuse me," Bea said when her phone range. She walked back down the hallway to answer it.

"This burger is so good!" I exclaimed after taking my first bite.

"Right?" Cynthia exclaimed. "That's why I said you guys had to try this place. It's not too greasy, with the perfect blend of grilled onions and mustard and the perfect amount of pickles."

"*Oh my God!*" Bea cried as she walked back in.

We all looked over at her and it seemed like she'd gone pale and was swaying on her feet.

I jumped up and ran over to her, placing my hand on her shoulder to steady her as I asked, "What happened?"

"A baby," she said softly.

"What baby?" I asked, not sure if she was talking about some new case or something else.

"We're getting a baby!" she exclaimed, her voice getting louder.

She peered up at me with a look of wonder and said, "A few months back ... one of the mothers we'd met with ... she, uh, changed her mind and decided to keep her baby. But now..."

"Now?" I prompted when her sentence trailed off.

"Now she changed her mind again. She gave birth just a few hours ago and there were some complications ... she was on drugs, so the baby came early, and his birthweight is low, but the adoption agency said he's doing good."

"So, you're getting a baby?" I asked, finally catching on.

"Yeah," Bea said, her eyes filling with tears. "I gotta go get Shannon and we've got to go to Vegas. Now!"

"Vegas?" Carmen asked.

"That's where they are," Bea said as she moved toward the door. "I have to tell work and get plane tickets and a hotel." She paused and looked back at us, then threw up her arms and said, "We're having a baby!"

"Wait, did you say his?" I asked. "It's a boy?"

"It's a boy!" she exclaimed with a laugh and then ran out the door.

We all stood there for a moment. Shellshocked.

Dylan was the first one to speak when she asked, "If

the birth mom changed her mind twice, could she change it again?"

"I guess she could, but we won't think about that," Cynthia replied. "We need to think positive thoughts and put that energy out into the universe."

"They're going to need ... everything," Amy May mused. "I know they were clearing out a room, but I don't think they went any further than that since they hadn't gotten any good news."

"We can do a baby shower," Carmen suggested. "But not like a traditional one. We'll contact everyone and let them know about the baby and ask them to assemble anything they buy, rather than wrap it, and we can set up the nursery for them so it's ready when they get home. Lila, you have a key, right?"

"Yeah," I said, getting excited at the prospect. "And they'll have to be there for a few days, minimum, until the paperwork is done, and the baby is well enough to leave the hospital."

"I have some duplicates of stuff that I meant to take back to the store but never got around to it. I'll bring those over and then we can make a list so that people have an idea of what they need."

"And now that we know it's a boy, we can ask Cade to paint the room."

"Jason will help," Amy May agreed.

"And I know Cade's parents will be happy to help in any way they can, too."

"Oh my gosh, this is going to be so much fun!" Carmen exclaimed.

"They'll be so surprised," I said with a grin.

"They aren't the type of people who would be upset by you guys going in there and doing all this behind their backs, without their input?" Dylan asked. "'Cause I would be."

Cynthia laughed and said, "Of course *you* would be."

"No, they'll be happy to have one less thing to worry about when they get back, and they'll be touched, I'm sure of it," I told her, and then added, "But, *noted* ... no surprises for Dylan."

"Okay, so I'll write up a plan and assign everyone their tasks," Carmen said, her phone in her hand to start on her notes. "We'll give them a chance to get packed and get to the airport, so how about we go by their house after work, Lila, just to get a lay of the land and decide what would work best in the room."

"Sounds like a plan," I told her.

"You're my kind of people, Carmen," Dylan added, and Carmen gave her a sunny smile.

Chapter Thirty-Seven

Bea and Shannon were fixtures in the Greenswood community, and the townspeople really showed up when Carmen reached out about them bringing home a new baby.

Not everyone assembled their gifts, but they sure were generous.

Cade, Jason and Bran helped by painting the room a pale gray and putting together the crib, changing table and dresser. Amy May and I were in charge of the bassinet for the master bedroom, the swing and highchair, which we pushed to the side of the living room and kitchen.

Carmen folded and hung clothes, oohing and aahing over every little piece of fabric. Bran kept shooting me looks every time she made a cooing sound, and I had to bite back laughter over the panic on his face.

"This looks so great," Cynthia said as she entered the nursery. She was carrying a stack of books and a large giraffe.

"You can put those on the dresser," I told her. "Cade's going to put the bookshelf together once he's done with the changing table."

"Oh, I can do it," she offered. "Putting together bookshelves is one of my specialties."

"Awesome."

Cade's ma was finishing up hanging the mobile, which was a bunch of animals that fit the safari theme we'd gone with, since Bea had told me that was the theme they'd decided on if they got a baby, no matter the gender.

I stepped back and looked around the room with a satisfied grin.

"Bea and Shannon are going to love it," I mused aloud.

"I think so too," Amy May agreed. "Have you heard from Bea?"

"Yeah, she told me they'd be home tomorrow and would let us know when we could come by to meet little Frederick."

"I'm so happy that Charlie is going to have a buddy

to grow up with, just like Cassidy did with Elena and Elin."

She put her arm around my waist and laid her head on my shoulder.

"It is nice having babies around again," I said.

"Yeah? You thinking of adding to the play group?" she joked, nudging my side.

I could almost feel Cade's ma perk up and pay attention.

I laughed and said, "I don't know about that. Sometimes I think it would be nice to have a baby, but then I look at Elin and Elena and how self-sufficient they are now, and wonder if I really want to start all over again, you know?"

"Oh yes, better than anyone," she said wryly.

"This is true."

"I know it's a decision for you and Cade to make, but I can't help imagining what a baby you two would make. He'd probably come out with muscles and long, perfect curls."

"That's a terrifying image," I said, smacking her arm lightly.

It didn't take long before we finished, and I was locking up as we all left the house.

"I can't thank you all enough for helping us do this for Bea and Shannon," I told the group. "It's going to take a huge load off of their shoulders and give them the opportunity to focus all their energy on Frederick, which is how it should be."

We all said our goodbyes and I promised again to let everyone know when Bea and Shannon were ready for visitors, then Cade and I got on his bike and drove out to the cabin.

We wanted to take a leisurely drive and Cade wanted to do some measurements on the old barn on his property, so he could get started on converting it into his shop. His parents had moved into their house, so Alani was living up at the cabin alone once more.

We pulled in between the two cars that were parked in the driveway and were instantly greeted by Rufus and CB.

"Hey, my babies," I said, crouching down to give them pets.

When I stood back up, they ran circles around Cade before following him across the grass to the house while I trailed behind.

I always loved coming out to the cabin. It was so peaceful and the house itself was beautifully done, although it did still have the feel of a bachelor pad rather than a home, but maybe it was time to change that.

"Cade, what do you think about…" My question fell off when I walked inside to see Cade standing in front of a kid who was maybe twenty and was looking fearfully up at my husband. "What's going on?"

"That's what I'm trying to find out," Cade said harshly.

I swear I saw the guy tremble.

"I'm, uh, a friend of Alani's ... she just went upstairs to grab something," the young man stuttered.

"Who are you?" Cade asked.

"Jon ... athon ... Jonathon."

"Hey, babe, what do you think about Italian for dinner?" Alani asked as she came down the stairs. When she saw her brother towering over Jonathon she froze for a moment, before running the rest of the way down and putting herself in between the two of them.

"Cade ... what are you doing here?" she asked, glancing quickly at me before focusing back on him.

"Last I knew, it was my house."

"Well, of course it's your house, I just meant that I didn't realize you were coming over."

"Obviously," he said, glaring at poor Jonathon.

"Cade," she admonished softly, before moving to stand next to Jonathon and placing her arm through his. "Cade, this is Jonathon, my boyfriend. Jonathon, my brother Cade and my sister-in-law, Lila."

"Hi," I said with a wave, while Cade's scowl just deepened at the moniker.

I moved to place a reassuring hand on Cade's back and said, "We were going to go take some measurements of the barn. Sounds like you guys are on your way out to dinner, so we'll leave you to it. Have fun."

I put pressure on his back to try and move him, but he stayed firmly planted until I whispered his name sternly.

We walked through the cabin and out the back door, the dogs trailing happily behind me.

"When are we taking the dogs back?" I asked him, hoping to distract him a bit.

"They like it here," he replied, walking so fast I had to practically jog to keep up.

"Well, sure, but they like it at the house too, and I'm sure the kids miss them."

"I thought it was a good idea to leave them here with Alani after Ma and Pops moved out. She obviously needs looking after."

"She's a young woman now, Cade. She's growing up and she's beautiful. Of course she's going to have relationships."

He stopped and turned so quickly I had to jump back in order not to run into him.

"Yeah, but *that guy*? He's scrawny and barely said two words."

"That's 'cause you wouldn't let him. Jesus, Cade, you

were practically beating your chest at him and daring him to piss you off. He looked like he was scared to death."

"Alani needs a man with courage. One who won't piss himself over a look."

"That's not fair, and you know it. Give the kid a chance. At least have a conversation with him before passing judgement." I stepped closer and wrapped my arms around his waist. "You know, pretty soon Lena's going to want to start dating. What are you going to do then?"

"Lock her away and start cleaning my guns on the porch every night."

I laughed and he grinned down at me.

"Sorry, you think Alani's mad?" he asked.

"I think she's probably used to you. But maybe next time you see Jonathon you say hello and crack a smile. Or at least don't scowl at him."

"I'll try," he said, bringing a hand up to brush my curls back off of my face. "You're the best thing that ever happened to me, you know that?"

"I do," I replied cheekily. "And the feeling is absolutely mutual."

"I heard what you and Amy May were talking about back at Bea's and you know I'm happy no matter what you want to do, right? If you want a baby, I'm down to try, as soon as possible ... The barn's free." His grin was contagious. "Or if you want to focus on Elin and Elena and growing them into the best humans they can be and then setting them free while we travel the countryside, I'm good with that, too. All I need is you by my side."

I leaned into him and closed my eyes as I hugged him tightly.

"Thanks, babe," I murmured, enjoying his warmth and scent surrounding me. "You're all I need!"

Well, him and cupcakes...

Epilogue

Jack Johnson was playing on the Bluetooth speakers, which were set up around the backyard. Ma and Pops had landscapers come in and make them a little backyard oasis with plenty of wildflowers, fruit trees, and a small koi pond with a bench and swing nearby.

The pig had been roasting on the spit all afternoon and was nearly done. The tables had been set up and were practically overflowing with food.

When I'd suggested they have a housewarming party, I'd envisioned a few of us all sitting in the dining room enjoying a nice meal while we gave them little gifts to welcome them to Greenswood.

I should have known better.

Ma had lived here a fraction of the time I had, and I

swear she'd met and invited the entire town ... and they all came.

I didn't know half the people here, but she was calling them all by name.

The kids were having a blast. Some of the kids they knew from school lived in this neighborhood and had been invited, so they, along with Cassidy, were all taking turns playing badminton in the back corner of the yard where Pops and Cade had set up a net. There was talk of a volleyball game later.

Seeing everyone together, and the kids so happy, I was struck again by how grateful I was that Cade's parents had decided to move here, even if it was part time. Actually, it was better that way, because that meant we could still go to Hawaii for visits too.

I moved through the yard, the skirt of my maxi dress swaying as I walked. Cade was over by the grill drinking beer and talking to Jason, Bran, and this guy named Hank who I'd only met briefly but I noticed his gaze kept getting snagged on Cynthia.

A small smile played on my lips as I walked over to my friend, who was laughing with her sisters.

"Hey, ladies," I said easily as I stopped next to them. "You having fun?"

"Yeah, your in-laws sure know how to throw a

party," Cynthia said, looking around. "And the house looks beautiful."

"I know, right?" I agreed. "They did such a great job making it their own in such a short amount of time."

"I have to admit this is my first time at a pig roast," Dylan said, her eyes going warily to the pig before quickly looking away. "I don't know if I'll be able to eat it."

"Oh, don't worry about it. There's plenty of other food," I assured her.

"It's just ... you know ... seeing the whole pig like that ... looking in its eyes ... it's a little more than I can handle."

"I understand. It takes some getting used to."

"Oh, look, there's Bea and Shannon," Cynthia said, looking over my shoulder.

I turned to see Ma rushing over and taking Fredrick from Shannon's arms.

"Aloha, Freddy," she gushed.

"I'm going to go say hi," I told them and went to do just that.

"Hi," I said as I moved to give each of them a hug. "How's motherhood going?"

They both looked tired but happy and smiled in response.

"So good. He does have a hard time staying asleep,

but we've been tag teaming and taking turns sleeping, so it's working out. I'm not sure how easy it'll be once Bea goes back to work full time, but I'm planning on working from home for the foreseeable future."

"If you ever need an extra set of hands, just let me know," Ma said, rocking back and forth as she cradled Frederick closely.

"We just may take you up on that," Bea replied, then took my hand and added, "And we have to say thank you again. You guys made our lives so much easier by getting the nursery ready."

"Yes, we love it," Shannon agreed.

"You guys don't have to keep thanking us. We were happy to help."

"I'm not going to stop for at least the next year," Bea said with a laugh, and I was met with a rush of emotion at how much better she looked and how happy she was. It was a far cry from where she'd been just a few months ago.

"Motherhood suits you," I said, giving her a kiss on the cheek before moving to help Amy May, who was walking outside with a large bakery box. "Oh, what do you have in there?" I asked.

"I've been testing out a few new recipes and I thought this one would be fun to test here. You can be my first subject."

"Goodie! I love being your Guinea pig," I exclaimed, reaching for the box as she lifted the lid. "Oh my, are those S'mores cupcakes?"

"They sure are."

"I love the toasted marshmallow on top," I said as I lifted one out and lovingly peeled back the wrapper.

The first bite was divine. A bit of graham cracker crust from the bottom, gooey, fudgy chocolate cake in the middle, and that delicious marshmallow on top made for the perfect blast of flavors.

"I've said it before, and I'll say it again ... *You're a goddess.*"

I finished the cupcake in three more bites and eyed the box like I was a predator, and it was my prey, but Amy May closed it and said, "You have to share."

I pouted and replied, "Spoilsport."

She leaned over and whispered, "I put a small box of four in Ma's fridge for you."

"Yay, I knew you loved me."

I made a mental note to go and hide that box in the back of the fridge next time I went inside. I'd hate for Pops to find it and think it was his.

"Of course. I'd never let you down."

"Thank you. Now, where's Charlie?" I asked, looking over to where Jason was still standing with the guys.

"She fell asleep, so Ma had me put her in the spare room."

Ma had not only put bunkbeds for the twins in one of the spare rooms, but a crib as well. She said it was just in case Amy May or Bea needed her help or came over, but I was pretty sure she was trying to manifest another grandchild.

"Who's that with Alani?" she asked as we moved toward the desert table.

"That's Jonathon, her *boyfriend*. He's been keeping his distance from Cade since they arrived, but I'm about to go make them interact. Maybe playing a game of cornhole would be a bonding moment."

Amy May snickered and said, "I doubt it. She's his little sister and this is the first guy she's brought around. He's bound to be a little protective."

"A little? Last time I thought he was gonna pick the poor guy up and literally throw him out."

"You can't force these things, Lila. They'll figure it out on their own."

"If you say so."

"I know so," she said. "Look at Cade and Bran. They used to hate each other and now they are almost friends."

I didn't tell her they were now on speaking terms because I *had* butted in and convinced Bran to put his fears aside and just apologize. I didn't *have* to always be right. Or rather, I didn't have to rub it in other people's faces that I was...

"Lila!"

I looked toward the house to see Carmen waving me over.

"Excuse me," I told Amy May, then went to see what Carmen needed.

"What's up?" I asked, then took a good look at her face and asked, "You okay?"

"Yeah, I'm good. I just stopped by the office to pick up something I'd forgotten and there was a message. So, I opened it, and it was a request from a man who's looking for his wife. He said she disappeared three years ago without a trace, and he's been contacting PIs in different cities across the county ever since trying to find her." She was speaking so quickly, she tumbled over some of her words. "He said money's no object, he just wants to find Starla, that's her name, so he's put in a request with us to do some digging here and in the Heights."

"Okay, sounds pretty straight forward. Why do you seem so upset over it?" I asked, watching as her eyes darted around.

"Because he sent a picture ... And, Lila, it's Cynthia."

"What?" I asked, automatically turning to find her in the crowd. "Are you sure?"

"Yeah, one hundred percent. He sent over a picture and there's no doubt that Starla is Cynthia. And all I could think on the way over is why she'd need a new identity. Like, what happened to make her run. And if she's not Cynthia, then who the hell is Dylan?"

My gaze shifted between Cynthia and Dylan, her supposed sister.

"It is strange, but we'll just sit her down and ask her," I told Carmen, putting my hand on her shoulder. "But not today, okay? Let's enjoy the party and then tomorrow we will talk it out and get to the bottom of things. I'm sure there's a simple explanation."

"Okay," she said, but she still looked frantic.

"You gonna be good?" I asked her.

"Yeah. I can be cool. It just freaked me out when I saw her picture."

"I bet. Go grab a glass of Chardonnay or something and enjoy the evening with your man."

She nodded and took off, passing Cade, who was on his way to me.

"Everything okay?" he asked when he reached me.

"Yeah, I think it'll be fine. Just a new case," I told him, wrapping one arm around his waist as he did the same and tucked me into his side.

"Nothing dangerous, I hope."

"Nah, I don't think so," I assured him, tipping my head back in invitation, which he accepted by dropping his head and brushing his lips against mine.

"*Aloha au ia 'oe*," he said softly as he lifted his head.

"I love you, too, Cade."

Lila will be back, but in the meantime, here's a glimpse at the first in a new series...

Starter Wife

Chapter One - Whitney

"And then I found out he was cheating on me and I couldn't believe it ... I mean, he'd left his wife for me. It just doesn't make any sense. He's such an asshole."

"Now, Amber, you know we need to refrain from the negative talk."

I *refrained* from rolling my eyes, but it was a serious struggle as I sat in the hard plastic seat with one hand holding a Styrofoam cup filled with day-old coffee and the other itching for my cell phone.

My therapist had recommended this group to me.

"Whitney," she'd said. "I think you'd benefit from being around women who are going through exactly what you are ...so you can see you're not alone. Sharing your story would be beneficial for you, and them."

I liked and trusted my therapist, so I'd given it a shot, but it hadn't taken five minutes before I realized she'd really missed the mark with this one.

No negative talk.

No bashing your ex.

No threats against your ex, or their new significant others.

No self-flagellation.

Those were the rules...

The twenty-something currently talking couldn't be further away from *like me* if she tried. The only thing we had in common was a cheating ex, but *hell*, I was pretty sure I had that in common with eighty percent of the population. That didn't mean I wanted to spend an hour listening to them whine, with nothing to show for it but a sore ass and the taste of bitter coffee.

Not wanting to be rude, but needing to escape as quickly as possible, I slowly leaned down to pick up my purse, then eased out of my chair and started toward the back of the room where the table with refreshments was set up.

They had stale donuts to go with the coffee.

Hoping the leader of the group would think I was going for a refill, or maybe to the bathroom, I exited the room without looking back. When the door closed behind me, I let out a sigh of relief and turned to walk toward the exit.

"Couldn't take it either, huh?"

I stopped, startled, and looked to the right to see two women sitting on a bench against the wall. The first had long, straight black hair and the most brilliant blue eyes I'd ever seen, while the other was small with the body of a bombshell and a smile that lit up the place.

I looked around briefly, and since I was the only other person there, deduced whoever had spoken had been speaking to me.

"Were you in the group?" I asked, throwing my thumb over my shoulder to indicate the door I'd just exited.

"Yeah, for about two seconds," the raven-haired beauty said as she stood up, stretching well above my five-foot, six-inch frame. "Then I ran screaming from the room, knocking over blondie in my need to escape."

With a giggle, the other woman stood up and reached out a hand.

"I'm Summer and this gorgeous Amazon is Margo."

I accepted her hand, shaking it briefly before replying, "Whitney."

"Recently divorced I assume," Margo said dryly.

"Guilty."

"Once Margo picked me up off the floor, we decided

to ditch this place and start our own group. Wanna join?" Summer asked sweetly.

"Oh, I don't know," I replied, thinking there was no way I could handle more of what I'd just endured inside.

"There's going to be alcohol," Margo said, piquing my interest.

"And junk food," Summer added, a hopeful expression on her face.

"*And* you can be as negative as you want. I'll even help you plan any revenge fantasies you may have."

I grinned at that. *I could see myself really liking Margo.*

"I can commit to one drink and we'll see from there."

"This is going to be so much fun," Summer cooed, almost causing me to back out right then.

"There's a place down the block, Campanella's. They've got a great happy hour and it's mostly an after-work crowd," Margo said as she checked her phone. "We should at least be able to get two rounds in before it's over."

"Perfect," I said, and headed to the door.

Once we were all outside, we turned our feet toward Campanella's.

"So, how long have you two known each other?" I asked, pulling my cashmere coat tighter around me.

The coat had been a Christmas gift from my ex,

Marcus, but I hadn't been able to get rid of it like I had most everything else. It was too warm and pretty.

"About ten minutes," Margo said with a chuckle.

"Oh, I didn't realize."

"Yea, I'm sure Margo wouldn't have looked twice at me if she hadn't mowed me down," Summer added good-naturedly.

"She's probably right. I was pretty intent on getting out of there as fast as possible and hopping in my car."

"Funny, isn't it. How we were all trying to get away from the group and now here we are heading out together. Three strangers with a common desire *not* to share our feelings with strangers," I said with a wry laugh.

"*I* don't mind sharing my feelings and I have a feeling we won't be strangers for long," Summer said as she opened the door to the restaurant and held it open for Margo and me.

It was like going into a portal. From the cool, quiet outside, to the loud and lively restaurant. The bar was full of smart-looking people in their suits and tailored jackets. The women had perfectly made-up faces and the men fresh haircuts.

It was the kind of crowd I'd loved when I was a young up-and-coming accountant. The kind I'd given up when I'd gotten married and stopped working so I could raise our family and keep house.

I ignored the pang of regret and followed behind Margo, who'd let the host know with a look that we were taking the last empty high-top table in the bar.

She obviously came in often and, really, you could tell she fit just by looking at her. With her long legs encased in perfectly straight slacks, high heels that would instantly leave me with a twisted ankle, and a well-cut blouse that was expensive without being flashy. This was obviously a restaurant full of her peers.

Summer, on the other hand, looked like a sunflower in the middle of a sea of black and navy weeds.

Unfazed by the fact she stuck out like a sore thumb, Summer hopped up on the bar stool and picked up the tapas menu as she looked around the room with a smile.

"Wow, lotta hotties here tonight."

I nearly choked on my laughter as I tried to get on the stool with as much grace as I could muster.

"If you go for the type," I said, glancing around. Because seriously, the men in this place were like carbon copies of each other.

"Just check with me before you go home with anyone," Margo said, without an ounce of jest. "I'll let you know if they're worth your time or not."

"Is that how it is?" I asked, infusing my tone with laughter so she'd know I wasn't judging.

"Let's just say I've been having a bit of rebound fun the last few months," Margo replied with a smirk.

"Here you are, ladies, a little something to get you started."

I glanced up as an attractive server placed a shot glass in front of each of us.

"What's this?" I asked.

"A gift from the guys at the bar," he replied, glancing behind him.

I followed his gaze to see three men watching us with matching grins, then turned back to Summer and Margo and lifted the glass in front of me.

"Let the games begin," I joked, getting ready to take the shot.

"Wait!" Summer shouted, startling me so badly I almost spilled the contents. "We should make a toast ... to the *Jilted Wives Club*."

"Is that what we're calling ourselves?" I asked, not sure if I liked the name, but willing to play along since it obviously made Summer happy.

"Yeah, how do you know we're jilted wives?" Margo asked.

"Based on the group session we were all supposed to participate in, I made an educated guess."

I looked at Margo and shrugged.

She rolled her eyes and said, "Fine ... to the *Jilted Wives Club*."

We all raised our glasses to each other, tapped them on the table, and did our shots.

The first meeting of the Jilted Wives Club had begun.

Acknowledgments

Thanks to my readers for sharing your love of this series with me and asking for more Lila and Cade.

Thanks to my mom, Ann, for being my first reader and offering your insight.

Thanks to Kristina, from Red Road Editing, for sticking with me all of these years.

Thanks to Allie, for this and all of the covers you've designed for me over the past decade.

Thanks to Lyn, Lori, Jennifer, and Kristi, for loving this series as much as I do and always saying *yes* to Beta reading.

Thanks to my ARC team for your dedication and continued support.

Always, thanks to my children, who give me unwavering support and keep me on my toes.

About the Author

Bethany Lopez is a **USA Today Bestselling** author of more than seventy works and has been published since 2011. She's a lover of all things romance, which she incorporates into the books she writes, no matter the genre.

When she isn't reading or writing, she loves spending time with family and traveling whenever possible.

Bethany can usually be found with a cup of coffee or glass of wine at hand, and will never turn down a cupcake!

To learn more about upcoming events and releases, sign up for my newsletter.

www.bethanylopezauthor.com
bethanylopezauthor@gmail.com

Follow her at https://www.bookbub.com/authors/bethany-lopez *to get an alert whenever she has a new release, preorder, or discount!*

Also by Bethany Lopez

Romantic Comedy/Suspense:

Delilah Horton Series

Always Room for Cupcakes - FREE

Cupcake Overload

Lei'd with Cupcakes

Cupcake Explosion

Cupcakes & Macaroons - Honeymoon Short - FREE

Lei'd in Paradise - Novella (Carmen & Bran)

Crazy for Cupcakes

Contemporary Romance:

Laugh, Swoon, and Fall in Love: Romance Series Starters Box Set

The Jilted Wives Club Trilogy

Starter Wife

Trophy Wife

Work Wife

Backup Wife

Accidental Wife - Preorder

Mason Creek Series

Perfect Summer

Perfect Christmas Anthology

Perfect Hideaway

Perfect Fall - Coming Soon

A Time for Love Series

Prequel - 1 Night - FREE

8 Weeks - FREE

21 Days

42 Hours

15 Minutes

10 Years

3 Seconds

7 Months

For Eternity - Novella

Night & Day - Novella

Time for Love Series Box Set

Time to Risk

The Lewis Cousins Series

Too Tempting

Too Complicated

Too Distracting

Too Enchanting

Too Dangerous

The Lewis Cousins Box Set

Too Enticing - Short

Three Sisters Catering Trilogy

A Pinch of Salt

A Touch of Cinnamon

A Splash of Vanilla

Three Sisters Catering Trilogy Box Set

New Adult:

Friends & Lovers Trilogy

Make it Last

I Choose You

Trust in Me

Friends & Lovers Trilogy Box Set

Indelible

Frat House Confessions

Frat House Confessions: Ridge

Frat House Confessions: Wes

Frat House Confessions: Brody

Frat House Confessions 1 - 3 Box Set

Frat House Confessions: Crush - Coming Soon

Women's Fiction:

More than Exist

Unwoven Ties

Short Stories/Novellas:

Contemporary:

Christmas Come Early

Harem Night

Reunion Fling

An Inconvenient Dare

Snowflakes & Country Songs

Fool for You - FREE

Fantasy:

Leap of Faith

Beau and the Beastess

Cookbook:

Love & Recipes

Love & Cupcakes

Children's:

Katie and the North Star

Young Adult:

Stories about Melissa – series

Ta Ta for Now!

xoxoxo

Ciao

TTYL

Stories About Melissa Books 1 - 4

With Love

Adios

Young Adult Fantasy:

Nissa: a contemporary fairy tale

Made in the USA
Columbia, SC
16 August 2022